THE NAMING OF MOTHS

SHORT STORIES OF MYTHS, MONSTERS AND MOTHERS

TRACY FELLS

First published November 2023 by Fly on the Wall Press
Published in the UK by
Fly on the Wall Press
56 High Lea Rd
New Mills
Derbyshire
SK22 3DP

www.flyonthewallpress.co.uk
ISBN: 9781915789099
Copyright Tracy Fells © 2023

Typesetting and cover design by Isabelle Kenyon, imagery Shutterstock.

A CIP Catalogue record for this book is available from the British Library.

For Graham and Robin.

With thanks to everyone who has supported and cheered on my writing ambitions.

CONTENTS

TEN GOOD REASONS

It struck me one day how easy it could be to kill my husband. I made a list of ten good reasons why I should execute the plan and then another list of ten appropriate scenarios.

"Not another bloody list, Trish?" said Geoffrey as I scribbled away in my hard-backed exercise book. I like the ones with the red stripe down the spine, coal black cover and blue ink lines inside. "You're obsessed."

I looked up the dictionary definition of obsessive and wrote a list of ten reasons why I couldn't possibly be classified as that.

Before my fiftieth birthday, I launched a tidy-up of the attic and found a hand-written note tucked into the back of an old diary. And so I recovered my first ever list: ten things I wanted to do before fifty. A bit overdue, I hadn't achieved any of them, but this simple collection of statements set me off on a fateful course, giving purpose, meaning and order to my life.

1. Visit Australia.
2. Swim with dolphins.
3. Write a novel.
4. Live abroad for a year.
5. Have an affair with a woman.

I placed the list inside my special box. Geoffrey doesn't know about this box; it's buried in a drawer with the rest of my 'women's things': *BIC* razors, tights, old lipsticks, a tape measure and diet books. The drawer was feminine territory – a Geoffrey exclusion zone – so my box was perfectly secure. All things precious were hidden there: the tiny plastic tag they had strapped around her wrist, the little white sock I'd squirrelled up my sleeve before they took her away. My one regret is I didn't take any photographs, so I only have that single memory, kept safe in my head.

I met Geoffrey long before the lists began. At twenty-four I'd been pretty naïve but pretty too, and six years without my beautiful baby girl. He'd sat on the edge of my desk in the showroom, seducing me with compliments and chocolate bars. As the Assistant Manager, he always wore a suit, smelled of *Old Spice* and smoked skinny cigars. He was ten years older and I thought him sophisticated, debonair and slightly dangerous. Every Friday, he took me out for a pub lunch followed by sex on the back seat of his demonstration car, parked down a quiet country lane. I enjoyed the lunches.

When I fell pregnant, he did the decent thing and we were all set to marry, two months before the baby was due. To my astonishment, he still went through with it, despite the miscarriage, so perhaps he really did love me back then. Oddly, the first time we had sex in a proper bed was on our wedding night – till then the backseat had always sufficed. It was his mother's double divan bed, which she grudgingly relinquished, like a toppled regent's throne, when we moved in. After three more miscarriages, Geoffrey had the snip, declaring, "What's the bloody point of carrying on with this misery?" Wish he'd talked it over first, but I guess he just wanted to protect me from future heartache.

I've grown to accept the punishment – my little angel hadn't forgiven me for deserting her – and my barren existence was deserved.

We had to live with Geoffrey's mother for most of our married life together. She couldn't live alone, *apparently*, and we couldn't afford a place of our own *apparently*. I was with his mother when she passed. She had just stopped breathing when the ambulance arrived – well that's what I told them as they tried to resuscitate her. Afterwards, all three of us, me and the two paramedics, chatted calmly over a nice cup of tea in the garden about the right to die in your own home.

That was five years ago and Geoffrey, as her only child, inherited her entire estate. Thankfully, he sold up the family home and we moved to Oak Wood Gardens, a genteel cul-de-sac where invisible occupants lined up pristine wheelie bins along the kerb on dustbin day. I thought I could be happy there.

From the kitchen sink, I watched a grey arrowhead of geese skim across the cloudless sky, calling to one another. They must be heading home. Behind me, the white board demanded attention: a new list. I reserved the kitchen board for my daily 'to-do' lists and things I mustn't forget. A good list is always ten in number: sometimes less can work, but ten is the optimum. Ten is a safe, solid and reassuring number. A week ago, Geoffrey inked a number eleven onto my kitchen list: "Get a life you sad ugly cow". I rubbed it off with a paper towel.

Last washday, squashing Geoffrey's golfing jumper (the colour always reminded me of those lemon tarts that only come out for kiddies' parties) into the washing machine, I sniffed perfume around the neckline. It had a sickly-sweet scent, but not cheap. And since I'd stopped wearing anything perfumed, eau de cologne or deodorant, years ago, I suspected another source. Brewing a pot of tea, I took out my notebook and started on the list of ten good reasons.

Earlier in the spring, Geoffrey had erected a shed at the bottom of the garden. It was more like a second home down there as he moved in an armchair, kettle, microwave; took the kitchen TV and even ordered a mini-fridge from one of my catalogues.

"I need sanctuary," he said. "Somewhere I can be alone to pot my seedlings in peace." This was my translation, though, in reality, he screamed something like: "I have to get away from you somehow – you crazy fat bitch!"

Geoffrey started spending all his evenings in the shed. And since he's become a permanent fixture there, I've had the house to myself to contemplate my list.

6. Learn to tap dance.
7. Get a puppy.
8. Put a thousand on red number ten at a casino in Monte Carlo.
9. Pose naked for a life drawing class.
10. Find my beautiful girl.

The telephone rang. I waited for the answer machine to kick in. Lauren again, from the showroom, asking when Geoffrey (she called him Mr Watkins) was going to be well enough to return to work. Her voice was a high-pitched, almost sonic, whine that only the young can get away with. She sounded blonde, pert and petite – just like I used to be. Did he take her out for Friday pub lunches? Perhaps she was too agile and gymnastic for poor Geoffrey to accommodate in the back seat of his Manager's company car. The lass would have to straddle his lap, hitch up her skirt across toned thighs, to avoid invoking one of his back seizures.

A week ago, I telephoned the show room about Geoffrey's absence, but then discovered I could send emails from his account and started emailing every other day to let them know he was "recovering but still feeling unwell."

This November, next month, she'll be thirty-six years old. I wonder if my daughter has done any of the things on my list. The Internet was my sanctuary and often I've thought about trying to find her, but it seemed from daytime TV that the etiquette was to wait for discovery, let your child seek you out.

Before the inevitable emotional and heart-tugging reunion in front of the cameras, I would appreciate a little time to tidy myself up a bit. I've been trying to lose weight. Sandra, the mobile hairdresser, has done a terrific recovery job on my home-dyed hair and I've started cycling in the living room. I picked out an exercise bike from a catalogue and the delivery man helped me put it together. I gave him a tenner and a packet of chocolate *Bourbons* (Geoffrey's favourites) for his trouble.

Now I was ready for that first momentous meeting. My new list was complete. Ten things I really will do. Already I'm achieving number one: Visit Australia. Lists should always be ticked off in order. Bag packed, I waited in the hall for the taxi transfer to the airport. Number two – swim with dolphins – should be easily accomplished during the same visit. I would start on the novel when I'm there and, if I found myself enjoying the life down under, I could push for number four and stay awhile. Who knows, I might get lucky with a Sheila and clear my top five before the return trip?

As I stepped outside, the first time in two years, the muted October sunshine warmed my skin. Autumn in England was the most glorious season. A time for beginnings, like starting a new term and hoping for better classmates (some friends even), but also an opportunity to turn back the clocks and recapture those lost dreams.

The taxi driver was a short stubby man with twinkling eyes and a lop-sided grin. He pointed to my one small carry-on bag with surprise, "Is this everything, love? Doesn't look much for a trip to Australia?"

I clambered into the spacious Mercedes (no expense spared for this trip, I'd even splashed out and bought a First Class ticket, one way) and explained, "I'm off to my daughter's wedding. She lives in Sydney and has promised to take me on a shopping spree

– a proper extravaganza before the big day."

The lies were easily woven because they really could have been true. There could've been an alternative reality where I'd kept my baby daughter – didn't have to give her up. A reality where she'd grown to become an independent, free-thinking woman. My little fibs were simply creative embellishments of what life should have been.

Craving new horizons and a better life, I was certain my daughter would have tired of England long ago and emigrated overseas. Australia. This is where I'd seek her out and my darling girl would be returned to me, for good this time.

"What a treat!" the driver replied with what sounded like genuine sincerity. "You are lucky to have such a loving daughter. And what about her dad, is he not travelling with you today?"

"Oh no." I smiled up at his reflection in the driver's mirror. "Geoffrey has already flown out. He wanted to go ahead to help with all the arrangements – you know, for daddy's little girl."

"Well, I wish you a very happy trip and blessings on your daughter for a joyous marriage. Do you have a list of all the places you plan to visit? My wife's brother lives in Melbourne and we never tire of visiting him and his family."

Well yes, obviously, but I'd already devised that list days ago. At the corner of the road, beside the post-box, I asked him to pull up so I could post the letter. In a day or two the lovely Lauren would receive the note and then set him free. Geoffrey could survive a few more days alone in his shed. I'd taped up his mouth to silence the expletives, strapped him to his favourite chair, and tucked around his mother's old crocheted blanket (the nights were getting chilly), but otherwise he was in fine form as I kissed him good-bye.

I let the driver prattle on as we cruised along the motorway, while I pondered on more important topics. All that remained was choosing a new name and then my resurrection would be complete. I fancied something more exotic than Patricia. Perhaps Angelina, Tallulah or Eveline, shortened to Eve to signify my regeneration... or even Phoenix, what an excellent name that would be. This fired an idea. Sinking comfortably back into the squeaky leather seat, I pulled out the notebook and pen from my handbag and began to write a list of ten good names.

VECTOR

Kevin watched in silence as Noah rolled the bird over with his bare foot. It was a black kite, a firehawk raptor. Kevin did everything in silence; he hadn't spoken since his mum had left almost nine months ago. *Long enough to whelp another bastard pup*, he'd overheard Grandma Sue tell one of the sheepdogs. The kite's belly plumage was the colour of milky coffee, a contrast to the dark brown of its back and wings. Only its beak, clenched shut, appeared truly black. Above them, the kite would have been a beautiful sight, soaring high on the thermals.

"Yeah, it's dead," said Noah, answering Kevin's heavy stare. "Poison, I reckon." He shrugged then looked towards the shade of a road-side acacia tree, where a sheep lay dozing on its side.

The sheep's swollen belly wasn't moving up and down like it should. Like the black kite, the sheep was dead. The buzzing cloud of flies that usually crowded a corpse was absent. Noah clicked his tongue, calling Gary, his bluey, away from the sheep. The dog ambled back to them, yawned and lay down at Noah's feet.

"Missus poisoned the carcass. No predator's going to pass up an easy meal," said Noah. He hung his head, causing the mass of wiry curls to fall across his eyes like a mask. "She's convinced them eagles are taking her lambs, and this poor bird has suffered instead. Missus be crazy."

Missus be crazy, was Noah's mantra. Kevin felt the weight of the old fella's words. They tied down Grandma Sue's shame while absolving her from punishment. She wasn't in her right mind. That's what the rest of the men on the sheep station muttered and mumbled behind her back. Her daughter had walked out into the bush, to follow Kevin's dad they all said. The Missus'

15

husband had scarpered years before that, taking his hat and best bitch, one of Gary's ancestors. Only Kevin, with his tight curls, squashed nose and skin baked brown like tree bark, remained at the homestead with his grandmother. But then at fourteen, and an abandoned *half-breed bastard*, he had little choice. Kevin pushed a tear away with his finger. He cried for the poisoned kite, its talons curled in death, its long, forked tail feathers stiff and flightless, and he cried for his mum.

In the acacia tree a second kite waited. "There's the female, probably its mate," said Noah. "Hope they haven't got chicks to feed. That's a tough job to do alone." He picked up the slack body of the dead bird, carried it over to the sheep. "Fetch a shovel from the jeep, Kev. Don't want to risk losing any more creatures."

Kevin knew about the firehawks; how they loved wild fires, but Noah started on a story anyway as he scraped and scratched out a shallow grave in the parched red dirt. He stopped between breaths to try and straighten his back. "I've never seen it, but my old fella did — before we came to your family's station. A wildfire raged for three days and nights, scorching everything in its path. Ten miles wide it spread, then weakened as flames licked the bush bare and came to a narrow creek, which formed a natural fire-break. The mister rejoiced that his prayers had been heard. The fire wouldn't make it to the homestead. They were saved."

Kevin nodded, hands deep in pockets — his stance mirrored that of the station workers each morning, eyes half-mast, as Grandma Sue shouted out the jobs for the day. He knew how Grandma Sue feared the dry winds that whipped slates off the roof, always listening for the crackle of untamed flames, scanning the flat horizon for the rose tint of dawn that shouldn't be seen in the middle of the day. They were too far from the nearest town; could never pump water quickly enough from the reserve tanks to douse a fire before help came. A wildfire would eat them up as easily as a raptor swooping up a running hare.

"Like shooting fish in a barrel," Noah said. "A wildfire is the firehawk's salvation. When a fire is dead, then the feasting is over."

But the firehawk was clever. Noah mimed a bird, diving with his arms outstretched, fingers splayed like feathers, sweeping up a smouldering branch. It flew to a dry area of bush and dropped its load. If the firehawk had chosen its torch well, then flames sparked, fuelling a new fire, hungry to consume everything in its path, and chasing out more prey.

Noah stared out across the flat dry bush towards the west. "Can you smell that, Kev?" He sniffed long and hard through his large fleshy nose. "Like roasting meat?"

Kevin shook his head.

"We'd best head home. Missus be going even more crazy if I don't bring you back by dusk." With a further click of his tongue, Noah headed for the jeep, the shovel swinging at his side. Kevin and Gary followed obediently at his black heels.

From her vantage point, the black kite watched them leave.

Noah let Kevin drive the last mile home, for practice. The jeep rocked and rolled, in and out of the dirt track potholes. Kevin gripped the wheel tight with both hands. His white soled trainers slipped on the pedals, making him fret over how Noah managed the jeep in bare feet. Noah never wore shoes or socks, preferring to feel God's earth beneath his toes. Kevin wasn't sure which god or spirits Noah favoured, guessing the old fella hedged his bets, particularly around Grandma Sue.

Noah snatched at the steering wheel, sharply tugging it towards him and causing the jeep to arc sideways. An open top pick-up sped past, throwing up red dust, the woman driver's face stared out, pink and startled, as she mouthed some obscenity. The jeep juddered to a stop and Kevin almost slid off his seat. The sky to the west glowed orange, as if the sun was setting early.

Kevin happily shunted across to the passenger seat as Noah took charge again. Gary jumped up to stand on his lap, nose glued to the gap in the window, claws gripping for purchase through his shorts and anchoring into flesh. Kevin chewed on his lip, making no noise despite the sudden surge of pain. He'd made a promise and he intended to keep it. He wouldn't make a sound, nor utter a word to anyone, not even Gary or Noah, until Mum came home. Came home for good.

Before Mum had left, there'd been words. Lots of words. Mean, cruel, spiteful words. He'd listened from his bedroom as Grandma Sue had catalogued Mum's failings: Kevin had been one of them – the chief one. That same night, he'd lain motionless under the covers when Mum knocked lightly on the door. Stayed silent when she softly called his name. Pretended to be asleep when Mum came into his room and kissed the top of his head. His silence had made her leave.

He was to blame.

Grandma Sue clearly thought the same, accepting Kevin's vow of silence as a fitting punishment and rarely addressing any comments to him directly. Instead she communicated via Noah, who took charge of Kevin's day-to-day existence and needs. She no longer insisted he went to school, so Kevin spent every day in Noah's company. With Gary, they took the jeep out to scout the station for sickly sheep, to fix fences and check on the water troughs. Around the homestead, they tackled the chores and jobs the other station hands considered beneath them, like stocking the larder, feeding the dogs and unclogging the dunnies. Noah didn't question Kevin's silence, continuing to fill the absence with his own chatter and stories. Gary accepted his ear scratches and belly tickles, and had only ever listened to Noah's commands anyway. Kevin was content because he had a plan. If Mum hadn't returned by the time he turned sixteen, then he was going to leave the station and find her. If she didn't want to come home, that would be okay, at least they'd be together. Then he would talk non-stop and fill the gaps of all that she'd missed.

The benefit of being on the outside of conversations was how easily adults forgot Kevin. They kept on talking in his presence, assuming silence meant he never listened either. He could see Grandma Sue's skinny outline through the mozzie screen hung across the kitchen doorway. She ran a hand over the spikes on her scalp as a torrent of words hit Noah, who was backing up towards the porch and freedom. Grandma Sue kept her white hair short, shaving it back to a snowy fuzz at the end of each month, and in silhouette with her canvas slacks and shirt she looked like a bloke. She was talking about Kevin, and shouting about the woman who'd called on her that afternoon. The same woman that had almost run them off the road earlier.

"Wants me to send him back to school. Stupid bitch. He can read and write, what else does he need to learn? What's the point of going to school when he don't talk? How's that going to work?"

There was a pause, presumably for Noah to respond, but Kevin could only hear Grandma Sue's voice, sharp as vinegar. "Selective mutism, she says. And I told her I bloody know what's wrong with him, tell me something useful. Like where's his mother? And who the fuck's his father? That's what I want to know. And when are they coming to fetch him?"

Noah must have said something, as Kevin could make out a contrasting tone, an exchange of softer words lowered beyond his hearing. What were they talking about, that they wanted to keep between them? Then Grandma Sue's voice rose again to dominate. "Don't be such an old woman. I've been on the radio for the last hour. It skirted Wattle Creek and veered northeast. Okay, we're basically sitting on kindling but it's not going to touch us. It can't reach this far. There's only scrub and nothing to burn between us and Hanson's station."

Fire. That's what Noah had smelled back where they'd found the dead kite. That explained the colour of the western sky. Not an early sunset, but the glare of burning bush. Kevin's heart was louder than his breathing. The homestead, stacked together from slats of wood, was no sanctuary, no safe harbour from a travelling wildfire. It would crackle and spit, like a steak on the griddle.

"Missus be crazy." Noah tugged on his smoke, inhaling through tunnel nostrils. "She dare call me an *old woman*. We should get to town before it's too late. We stay and the wind changes, then we is all trapped." Gary settled at Noah's feet, now squashed into his only pair of leather boots. Kevin stared at Noah's hidden feet. That wasn't a good sign. Noah was preparing to leave. He wouldn't go without them, *would he?*

Only Noah's jeep was parked up outside the bunkhouse. The rest of the station hands had already left, taking the dogs. Tyre tracks in the dirt road twisted and twined like mating snakes. The veranda door swung open behind them, kicked out by Grandma Sue as her hands were occupied with the shotgun she kept in her office. She lifted the long gun to her shoulder, sighting it towards the crooked gum tree that provided the only natural shade near the homestead.

She fired once, then again. Kevin covered his ears as the thunderous claps reverberated, making him wince with pain. Noah swore, dropping his smoke and stubbing it out with the heel of his boot.

The black kite watched them from one of the top branches.

Grandma Sue moved to reload, but Noah moved quickly, pulling her arm down. "Leave her be, Suzanna," he said with surprising gentleness. "She's lost her mate."

From her perch, the kite launched forwards, wing tips stretching above them like storm clouds. She soared over the roof of the farmhouse, carrying something in her talons. A stick no wider than her body.

Kevin thought of Noah's firehawk story. The black kite was a vector, carrying burning twigs to start new fires and flush out more prey.

The kite dropped her load, then rose higher and higher. Kevin tried to follow her spirals, but the sun made his eyes water and blink as she disappeared into the haze. The smouldering stick fell onto the roof and bounced and rolled into the bone-dry wooden eaves. Grandma Sue laughed and sank to the ground, still clutching the shotgun.

Flames jumped and jigged, feasting hungrily and growing taller, stronger with each second. Grandma Sue's manic cries turned to shrieks, and Kevin leapt back, tripping over Gary and thudding into Noah. The fire took hold at a breath-taking speed. Within minutes, the roof turned orange and gold, streaked with plumes of black. The flames crested over the eaves, an unstoppable tidal wave of destruction fuelled by the building's wooden frame. The fire was alive. It sucked up all the air, stealing his grandmother's words; rendering her mute and silent.

Noah wrapped his arms around the woman's chest, scraping her backside and streaking her trousers with rust-red stains as he dragged her towards the jeep. She let the shotgun fall away, didn't struggle or kick in protest. When Kevin looked into her eyes, all he saw was the reflected fire.

"Missus be crazy," said Noah, as he and Kevin hauled her

into the back of the jeep, "but she's all we got."

Noah's hands shook as he gave the keys to Kevin. "You have to drive. I'll sit with her."

Gary leapt onto Kevin's lap, licking at the boy's neck. It wasn't ideal to drive with the dog standing guard, claws pricking his legs, yet Kevin found it a comfort. They were all safe. He knew where to go.

Kevin drove slowly, weaving between the potholes. Grandma Sue lay on the back seat, her head scrunched against Noah's leg. She was pale and silent. He called out to them both, his voice calm and controlled, "We're going to find Mum."

Swirls of red dust trailed the jeep as Kevin's confidence grew and he picked up speed. The fake sunset raged behind them, engulfing the bunkhouse and barn. There was no sign of the black kite. Kevin hoped it too was safe, out searching for a new mate. Ahead he could see for miles, the road was empty, the sky a blank canvas.

THE NAMING OF MOTHS

"He is my son, I created him." Miss Bethan's words fall softly, like a blessing.

Sofia leans closer to hear the old lady, her long black hair falling against Miss Bethan's nightdress. A noise scratches from inside the pleated shade of the bedside lamp, where a moth has become trapped. She cups it quickly within her palms, ignoring the heat of the bulb.

"Let me see," Adam calls out. He has been sitting at his mother's bedside since midday, never once leaving her. His eyes shine. He wants to name the moth.

Sofia lets him peep into her hands. The moth has distinctive markings, black bands stretched across crimson wings. A common species for the time of year, though usually found during the day.

"Cinnabar." He names it correctly, grinning with pride. Adam remembers every moth, even the ones Sofia has only described from memory. He can learn, she thinks, despite what his uncles say – the same uncles who gather in Miss Bethan's house, waiting for the old lady to die.

Sofia lets the moth escape into the garden, then shuts the window, clicking the latch tight. "Did you open the window, Adam?"

He shakes his head. Adam does not lie.

"I opened it." A woman's voice answers. One of the uncles' wives has joined them upstairs. A woman with dark eyes and the shadow of a moustache framing her top lip, hair tightly combed back from her face. She drapes a towel over the dressing table mirror. "It stinks in here." The woman pinches her nose – an unnecessary mime – then is gone again.

23

Miss Bethan is incontinent and the July air is humid. Sofia no longer worries about how life smells; if she breathes in too deeply all she tastes is ash. Miss Bethan's milky-blue eyes no longer see, but they open at the sound of an unfamiliar voice.

"Sofia," Miss Bethan begins slowly, "I would like to talk with you. Alone." Her breath struggles like the last flames of a dying fire.

Sofia understands it won't be too much longer and gently nudges Adam. "Your mother needs to rest now. Kiss her goodnight, then wait for me in the garden."

Adam doesn't move from his chair.

Miss Bethan quietly repeats Sofia's request and Adam stands. He kisses his mother's cheek then shuffles to the door, stooping so as not to bang his head. Once the boy has left, Sofia sweeps the soil from the chair to sit beside her employer. It takes some minutes for Miss Bethan to recover enough strength to continue.

She asks Sofia to do a terrible thing. Something a mother should never ask.

Sofia sits on the bed, takes Miss Bethan's hand. A blue vein pulses through the old lady's skin, which ripples over prominent bones. Her palm is cool and dry. Miss Bethan's husband, Isaac Whiteman, had long since passed when Sofia first came to live with the old lady. Sofia believed her English was good and would secure her employment. Her thesis tutor, Professor Assaf, had always encouraged her to read and discuss the latest journal papers in English. Twisting his ghost-white moustache, brown eyes serious for once, he had even proposed she submit a paper based on her doctoral research to *Nature*. Entomology was her field, Lepidoptera – moths her speciality. He encouraged her to consider the UK, which he assured her would be welcoming. They'd invite her to teach at one of the prestigious universities, and she could continue her research there.

Ultimately, she had waited too long to act on Professor Assaf's proposal, misjudged the escalation of events, and left it too late for his endorsement.

After the university suffered a direct attack, her research lab ground to rubble, Sofia accepted there was nothing left to stay for. On the day a rocket targeted the university, the fire chose to absolve her, let her slip free, while it rampaged like a rabid animal, devouring both the living and the dead. It consumed the newly-emerged Striped Hawk-moth larvae as they gorged on hand-picked leaves. It flamed the pupae, expectant in their glass cabinets like paper-wrapped Mummies. It burned through the Department of Zoological Sciences, including Professor Assaf's office. All Sofia could salvage was his promise of the dreaming spires of England.

A soldier promised to help her across the border, once she'd paid him of course. With her sisters and mother gone, what was the point in hoarding the money she'd saved? When the truck was hit by a shell, the soldier ran, abandoning Sofia and the others to the burning wreckage. She didn't blame him. He still had a family to run home to. Thrown from the truck by the blast, somehow she crawled free of the inferno, her body alight like a slithering beacon.

When she finally reached the UK, her English was considered good enough to cook and clean for an old woman. Sofia was just another immigrant whose qualifications earned scant respect without the references and paperwork to support her claims. The dreaming spires were just dreams. Realising this, she gratefully accepted Miss Bethan's offer of a room, along with the role of unpaid housekeeper and carer.

Adam still lived with his mother and Sofia quickly understood he couldn't look after her alone. Over six foot tall and broad as a doorway, with mud-brown hair and eyes to match, he looked only a few years younger than Sofia – even though by twenty-nine, Sofia had lived hard enough to look twice her age. Despite his size, Adam was like a child, an innocent in a world he barely knew or understood.

Miss Bethan's eyes are wide and staring, her voice shakes as she begins: "I was so lonely, after Isaac. I summoned Adam, but out of love, you understand."

The old lady's words echo with shame. Was she seeking Sofia's forgiveness? Surely, only Miss Bethan's God could grant that? She continues, telling how she breathed life into Adam. How she created her son. Her story was incredible, but Sophia had seen so much wickedness out there, beyond Miss Bethan's net curtains and best china. There must be a balance: Adam was that balance.

One of the uncles arrives to relieve Sofia. Miss Bethan is silent, eyes closed as if she is sleeping. He grinds his foot into the carpet. "That dumb lump leaves dirt all over the house. How do you stand it?" The man is talking to Sofia. His overlong silver hair makes her think of a wolf. She squeezes past, but he holds her arm and doesn't let go. He makes Sofia take an envelope, stuffed with cash.

He doesn't look at her, mumbles instead at the carpet. "Tomorrow we'll take her from here. I'm sorry, but there is no longer a job for you." He swallows quickly, as if this helps to get it over with. "We are grateful for all you've done. This should help you, while you find something else."

He means, "Find somewhere else to live." Sofia has lived

with the old lady for almost two years, ever since she first
arrived in England. Miss Bethan's garden is fragrant with shrubs
and flowers attracting the nectar hungry butterflies and bees.
At dusk, the bats skim the half-light for insects. The moths
come later to feast in the moonlight. Each moth she discovered
was named and shared with Adam. Sofia taught him how to
recognise their markings. Here she had found sanctuary, and
healing. Now this is what she must leave behind: Miss Bethan's
garden.

And Adam.

"He's not her real son, you know." The man's breath is
stale, tainted with the echo of his last meal. "She couldn't have
children, so it's impossible. We don't know where he came
from."

"Adam came from the earth," says Sofia.

"He's just another waif with a sob story that Bethan fell
for. He can't stay either." The man seems to hiss at her. "Social
services can look after him. He should've been in care years ago.
Can't even read or write for pity's sake."

Sofia pulls away from his grip, tucks the handkerchief Miss
Bethan gave her into the pocket of her apron. She thinks of
Adam, alone in the world. Maybe Miss Bethan's request was a
kindness after all.

When Sofia hurries through the kitchen, she feels them not
looking at her. The waiting relatives sip coffee from Miss
Bethan's bone china, and Sofia knows once outside they will
talk of nothing but her face.

The door of the downstairs bathroom is open. The woman
with the moustache is refreshing her lipstick in the only mirror
left uncovered. She is talking loudly to nobody in particular.
"What was Bethan thinking, bringing that sort of girl into her

home? Along with that lurching creature. At least poor Isaac is no longer here to see his wife's shame." She pauses, pouting her lips together like a fish, sees Sofia watching but still continues, "He wouldn't have tolerated this refugee circus – not for a minute."

Outside, Sofia closes their world behind her, breathes in the lingering scent of lavender and the Buddleia bushes, flower heads drooping like bunches of purple grapes. Adam waves from the bottom of the narrow garden, waiting where they've set the moth trap. The flutter and flap of wings from the trap greets her as she approaches. Adam holds out his cupped hands to show her his prize.

"Lime Hawk-moth," he says, then lets the moth fly free. From the back pocket of his jeans, Adam pulls out a spiral notebook and a blue biro. "Do you want to write it down?"

This is their nightly ritual: the naming of moths. Sofia records each species in the notebook in careful print. Adam repeats each one, learning the new names.

"No," she says softly, looking back to the house where Miss Bethan's room is now dark. Sofia waits for the wailing to begin, the sound of grief, but the house remains still and silent. As she tugs at the buttons on Adam's shirt, done up to his neck, her fingers shake.

"What are you doing?" he asks like a child.

"I need to honour your mother." Sofia wipes at her eyes and struggles to pull open his shirt. How is she going to tear it with her bare hands? "It's her custom. You need to rip it here, above your heart."

Adam obeys and easily tears the fabric with his fingers. There are marks on his chest, letters written in black ink. Sofia pulls open his shirt.

"What have you done?" she whispers, her fingertips tracing the names that cover his skin.

Ruby Tiger. Cinnabar. Dusky Peacock. Brimstone. Rosy Footman. True Lover's Knot.

"Mamma helped me," Adam says brightly. "I told her the names and she wrote them... before she got sick." He rolls up his left sleeve. "Look, this one I had to write myself, Mamma told me how. I put it here so I could see it every day." Adam speaks the name as her fingers flit over his skin, "Hummingbird." He grins. "It's your favourite moth."

"Yes, it is."

"Because it hovers like a hummingbird."

Sofia nods. He learnt this from her, as Adam has never seen a hummingbird. Miss Bethan didn't keep a television or computer, not even a radio, in the house. She wanted Adam to remain an innocent.

"I didn't know you could read," Sofia says quietly.

"I just remember the shapes and how they sound, that's all." Adam rubs his arm. "Mamma has numbers, here on her skin. I wanted numbers too, but she said I should pick names I love. I chose all our favourites."

"Your mamma told me names are important." Sofia can see he is listening carefully as she speaks. "When she first came here after the war she had another name. Did you know that?" Adam shakes his head. "She was sent to live in Wales with her sister. They both chose new names, believing their own sounded too foreign." Sofia realises he will understand little of what she is telling him, but feels he needs to learn something of Miss Bethan if she is to keep her promise.

He touches the left side of her face, where the burn scar has calmed, turning almost white. When her hair grew again she didn't cut it, letting a mask of tangles cover her cheek and neck, but the scar tissue scalds most of her shoulder, snaking over her chest, back and arm.

Phoenix, was another favourite moth, though disappointingly dull in its subdued camouflage colours.

"There are more letters here." Adam lifts his own heavy fringe to reveal three symbols, thick and black, etched into his forehead. "Mamma says they were there when I was born. Can you read them?"

"I think they are Hebrew," answers Sofia.

Miss Bethan had explained how the three characters spelled out *Truth*. On the back of Sofia's hand, Miss Bethan had weakly traced out the shape of the character that she was to erase. Then she pointed to the drawer where Sofia found the handkerchief. "Remove it and *Truth* becomes *Death*," Miss Bethan told her. "Adam will not feel anything. He will simply crumble into dust, cease to be."

"The letters — what do they say?" Adam's wide eyes beg. "Did Mamma tell you?"

Sofia pulls the crisp white handkerchief from her apron and spits on it, like her own mother used to do. "It is your name," she lies and reaches up to his face. "Here, let me wipe this away." Sofia presses the handkerchief to his mouth. "You have a smudge of dirt."

Standing on tip toe Sofia kisses Adam on the lips. She expects him to taste of the cold, damp earth, but instead he is warm and sweet. His skin smells like Miss Bethan's garden after spring rain.

"Did you like that?" she asks.

"Yes." He is grinning.

"Good." Sofia knows he can only tell the truth. Adam was not created to lie.

Sofia points to the blue biro. "Write on me." She pulls up the sleeve of her sweatshirt to expose the paler skin on the underside of her arm. "Write the name of your favourite moth."

Adam's tongue pokes from his mouth as he thinks on this.

"There are too many to choose from!" Eagerly, he presses the pen to her skin.

The letters are wobbly, messy and the K is backwards. "Dark Beauty," reads Sofia.

He shuffles his feet, fringe falling over his brown eyes. "You are beautiful," he says.

Soon, she will have to explain how his mother has passed. Tell him he is free to choose his own name, if he wants to. Let him explore and learn what the world truly holds for the displaced and unwanted.

For now, she is content to name moths. "Go on," Sofia urges him, holding out both arms, "write as many names as you can. Every moth we've ever found together."

As he writes, Adam carefully names each one.

COPING MECHANISM

My replacement is early. The girl strides past the kitchen window, tall and willow-thin, taking the path around the side of the house to the back door as if she owns the place. Why doesn't she come to the front and ring the bell like anyone else?

Finn mewls like a kitten from his Moses basket on the floor. He's hungry, needing yet another feed, and the mewling will soon elevate to a piercing wail if I don't pick him up. But I don't want to breastfeed in front of her. I want to brew proper coffee, not flick on the kettle. I want to settle calmly at the oak table and pull out a tin of flapjacks, freshly baked that morning especially for our new houseguest. Milk is leaking through my T-shirt. I'm going to greet the au pair with damp circles around my nipples.

I call her a girl because she's ten years younger than me, recently graduated and starting her life. I call her my replacement because that's the intention: to replace an incompetent mother who can't even satisfy her baby's hunger. Finn fed less than an hour ago. I haven't had time to shower or stack the dishwasher or start a multitude of tasks I won't finish and he's hungry again.

"Hello, Mrs Cave?" The girl calls out, as the back door opens inwards. She doesn't knock, just walks straight in.

Our name is Cavell, but I don't correct her. "Hello, Agnes," I say, folding my arms across soggy breasts. "Please call me Hannah." Thankfully, Finn falls silent, giant blue eyes gaping up at her.

"Hannah," says the au pair, her mouth exaggerating the 'H'. "And this must be Finn." Her accent is Eastern European. Cruelly, I think of those feeble Hammer Horrors set in dark Transylvanian villages. Agnes smiles down at my son. "Can I hold him?"

She peels off knee-high black boots, bringing her down to my height. We look each other in the eye. Hers match mine, slate-grey flecked with blue. Ebony lashes and pale skin contrasts against her flushed red lips. Agnes doesn't smile at me. Swinging off her rucksack, her only luggage, she then swoops down to gather up Finn. He gurgles, a rare signal of contentment, and plump fingers reach for Agnes's long hair draping her shoulders like silk.

"Be careful," I warn. "It will really hurt if he starts tugging."

"Is no worry." Agnes bounces Finn in her arms. "He is strong little boy. Little man," she coos and kisses his nose.

"Coffee?" I scuttle to the sink. Fill the kettle. Drag an opened packet of Hobnobs down from the cupboard, my earlier breakfast. She should be doing this, I realise, making me coffee. Steven has brought Agnes into our home to look after me.

"I should do this," says Agnes. She hands Finn to me, then takes two mugs from the cupboard next to the Aga I never use. How does this girl know my kitchen? "Steven show me all around," she says, answering the question in my head.

I don't like how my husband's name sounds on her lips.

Steven, along with his mother, had called in and interviewed four candidates for the position of our au pair. That was the day after Finn rolled off his changing mat on the sofa when I left him, only for a second, to answer the phone. I didn't know babies could roll at that age. He didn't hurt himself, but that wasn't the point according to Steven and his mother.

"Agnes was by far the most suitable," he told me during a stilted Sunday lunch at his parents. I couldn't be trusted with cooking either.

"She spoke the best English," his mother chipped in, "and seems bright enough to cope with Finn."

Mother and son bowed their heads in unison, returning to plates of roast beef and Yorkshire puddings pooled with gravy.

Their unspoken accusations congealed, conspiring with the potatoes that huddled, cold and untouched, at the centre of my plate. Because I couldn't cope with Finn. Couldn't cope with keeping my son or myself fed, clean and happy. An au pair was their perfect solution for coping with me.

Finn fidgets, fights against my cuddle. His cheeks redden as he begins to cry again. "He needs feeding," I tell Agnes.

She picks up her rucksack, tosses back her hair. "Is no problem. I will go to my room." The replacement glances around my kitchen. "Then I clean up and make us lunch."

"Shall I show you to your room?"

Agnes shakes her head. There is still no smile for me. "Steven show me."

Of course he did.

"Do you think she looks like me?"

Steven doesn't look up from his iPad, flicks a finger across the screen. "I guess. But I didn't know you then."

"What do you mean?" I turn on my side. Watch my handsome husband as he continues to work in bed, another once strictly upheld rule overthrown by parenthood. Once upon a time, our marriage bed was for sex and sleep, in that order.

He taps his bare chest idly. "You know, when you were at college."

"You mean when I was younger – when I was her age." I slump back against the pillow. The clean T-shirt I'd put on for bed was already blotched with a milk stain. "I felt a right dairy cow when she arrived this morning. Stood there, massive udders squirting, no make-up and Finn on the floor like a workhouse baby, while she swans in, fairy-tale gorgeous, swishing her hair like Rapunzel."

Steven carefully places the iPad on his bedside table. "Why was Finn on the floor?"

I sigh, close my eyes before answering. "Finn was in his basket. The one your mother gave us, which I can carry from room to room so I never have to leave him alone."

He nods. Rubs the golden stubble dotting his chin. "She does look a bit like Rapunzel. Did you notice it goes all the way down to her bum?" Steven pushes away a loose strand of hair to kiss my cheek. "You could grow your hair long again, I'd like that."

Six months into the pregnancy, I'd cut my hair to shoulder-length – everyone said it would be more manageable when the baby came. At eight months, I took it even shorter to a box cut bob, sleek and stylish. Steven said he loved the new look. Called me a Yummy Mummy. Now I know how he really felt.

His hand is snaking up inside my T-shirt. "I also like these massive tits."

I'm trying not to let him see the tears. He hates it when I cry. Turning away, I feel him press into my back. His hardness was all it used to take. "Sorry," I mumble. "I'm still sore down there." Like most natural deliveries, I'd been cut to ease Finn's escape.

Steven withdraws his hand. He lies back and I hear him pick up the iPad. "Okay," he says quietly.

As I finally slip into sleep, Finn wakes in the nursery. Despite hugging the pillow close to my ears, I still hear his cries through the wall. I recognise the distinctive demand for food. He's hungry again. My body tenses, waiting for the click of Agnes' door. Surely she will go to him?

Steven is sprawled across most of the bed, squeezing me to the very edge. Blonde lashes twitch as he dreams. Finn's cries loop into a continuous screech. Clearly Agnes, like Steven, can sleep undisturbed through Finn's vocal assaults, as there's no sign of any movement from her room.

"You're his mother," Steven had said to me when we first came home from the hospital. "You're instinctively tuned to his frequency."

Slipping out from my warm cocoon, I shiver as the cool night air slaps me fully awake. Finn's screams shake the house. Only the dead could sleep through this. Steven brushes a finger under his nose but doesn't wake. My husband and our new au pair are clearly in league with the dead.

Over the following weeks, I fall into a routine with Agnes. I become Finn's wet nurse. Feed on demand, then rest and stuff myself silly when Steven is out. Agnes tackles everything else: changing and bathing Finn, cleaning the house, shopping, sorting Steven's dry cleaning (two suits a week) and all the cooking. She sings as she works, melodies I don't recognise and words I can't understand. "Romanian folk songs," she tells me. "My grandmother taught me." My guess at Transylvania was close.

One afternoon, I'm curled on the sofa drifting in and out of sleep. Finn is feeding every two hours now without fail. Exhausting, but at least he's settled into a predictable pattern. With the TV chattering in the background, I dream of Helen, my elder twin and spitting image. She's trying on my favourite white skinny jeans, spinning round to admire her perfect bottom in the full-length mirror of our bedroom. I swear she's wearing my Jimmy Choo heels; the crimson pair Steven bought me after the first positive pregnancy test. Her long fingers twist a necklace around her neck, pale pink pearls like the ones I wear for Steven when I want to have sex. I'm usually naked when I wear those pearls.

The dream is a lie. I can no longer squash my flabby baby belly into those jeans and they wouldn't fit Helen either. Helen died in a car accident when we were ten.

Something touches my shoulder. I smell coconut, the synthetic tang of manufactured sweetness. Agnes leans over me, long hair tickling my cheek. The coconut scent is shampoo; is she using mine? I'll check her bathroom tomorrow when she takes Finn out in his buggy. She springs back as I sit up quickly, swinging my legs off the sofa.

"You have tattoo," says Agnes.

I pull my T-shirt back in place to cover the fraying bra-strap. "Yes, I've had it since I was a teenager."

"Just one?"

"Yes." Automatically, I reach to scratch my left shoulder. I can't feel the tattoo, but this action is always comforting.

"And Steven does not mind?"

Agnes is wearing a pair of white jeans; clinging like a second skin to her slim legs. "No," I answer, but then hesitate. This girl works for me. I should tell her to mind her own business. "Steven loves it."

"What is in bird's mouth?"

I'm eye level with her crotch. Staring at the white skinny jeans. Is she wearing my clothes? I wonder how to pose this question. "The bird – it's a dove. In its beak is the letter 'H'." The dove is painted with white ink, the letter blood red. I chicken out and say, "I have the same pair of jeans."

"H for Hannah?"

Helen had always been the better dancer. She'd been picked to dance the Sugar Plum Fairy in our ballet school's Christmas performance of The Nutcracker. I'd sulked at home with Auntie Rachel, pretending I had a tummy ache so I didn't have to watch my sister prance about in her tutu, hand-stitched with silver sequins that sparkled like diamonds. I wasn't in the car when the lorry hit Dad's BMW head on. Wasn't there when the fire took hold, trapping Mum and Helen.

But I'm not going to tell her any of this. "Yes, the H is for Hannah." Standing, I expect Agnes to step out of my way, but she is so close I can feel her breath. She must have switched the TV off while I slept. The house is quiet. Eerily quiet. I realise why. "Where's Finn?" There's a tremor of panic in my voice.

Agnes rolls her eyes towards the ceiling. "He sleeping upstairs."

On cue, the silence ends with Finn's sharp cry. Two hours to the minute from his last feed. I sigh. "He *was* sleeping."

Agnes shrugs. "He is hungry."

He's always fucking hungry, I want to scream in her face. I could ask her to move. Tell her to fetch Finn. Give her an order and expect instant obedience. Her grey eyes watch me for a moment. She sinks onto the sofa, picks up a magazine from the coffee table.

Breathing heavily, I step over her legs. After feeding Finn, I'm going to check the wardrobe, dig out my white jeans. With the constant milk production, I must be losing weight. Maybe I can fit into them again.

Finn turns his head, spits out my nipple. Stubby fingers push my breast away as he screws up his eyes and screeches his frustration. Turning him round, I try the other breast and he latches on like a lamprey. The sucking reflex is immediate; his lips tug and tug, pulling me further and further away from myself. Nails scratch the dimpled skin around my nipple as he rages against the slow supply. This mother-baby nursing experience is supposed to calm us, bond us close, but Finn hasn't read the baby books. This is his battlefield. After several minutes, he's drained me dry and wriggles to get free. I see us in the bedroom mirror. A pink-faced baby squirms in the pale arms of a bony wraith. My hair is dull and tangled, eyes aching. I'm a nightmarish hag skulking in the shadows, about to steal back the changeling baby.

In the kitchen, Agnes is talking on our telephone. Twisting a strand of raven-black hair, she laughs, a low, deep laugh from the back of her throat. Finn is quiet, sucking on my finger. This has appeased his anger but I doubt it will keep him happy for long. He could be teething and not hungry for once.

Steven's mother believes I pander to Finn. "He's just teething, Hannah. Rub a little brandy into his gums. That always worked for Steven," she shared at her last visit. "Have you tried Calpol?"

"He's too young for Calpol," I replied, glancing at Steven. But he and his father were heads down at the kitchen table, immersed in the Sunday supplements. The men have evolved their own coping mechanisms.

"Nonsense." Steven's mother snorted. She started searching through the cupboards, tutting each time the contents displayed my failings. "I'll pick you up a bottle from the chemist's next time I come over."

Agnes sees me, but continues her conversation. Several weeks under our roof and her accent is fading fast – she's starting to sound like me, a middle-class suburban housewife. In profile, I imagine this is how my younger self once looked. Shining eyes. Open lips flushed and ready to devour everything life has to offer. The symmetry of her bone structure is familiar. She could be me. An odd thought makes me shiver. She could be Helen. This is exactly how Helen would look at twenty-two.

Agnes blinks slowly, looks directly at me. "She's here now. Do you want to speak to her?" Agnes holds out the telephone. "It's Steven," she says. Not *your* husband or even Mr Cavell, but Steven.

I snatch the phone. Before I can say anything, he's gushing on about some deal he's pulled off. We need to celebrate and he's invited his parents over for dinner on Saturday night. He's giving me plenty of warning: Saturday is three whole days away, so I have time to sort out a menu for Agnes to prepare. Plenty of bubbly – the deal is a big one – we don't need to scrimp, so I can get the proper stuff. Scurrying to the lounge, the phone propped on my shoulder and Finn still in my arms, I tell him Agnes is a thief.

"Don't be an idiot, Hannah," says Steven, "of course she hasn't taken your jeans. She's just got a similar pair."

I hiss into the phone. "How could she afford the same ones? I looked in the wardrobe – they're not there! I'm sure other stuff is missing too. That cream top you like, with the diamante straps. My furry ankle boots."

"Hannah." He's using the same tone he reserves for Finn and little dogs, mock cutesy. "Have you looked everywhere? In the washing basket?"

For a pair of ankle boots? I want to shout back. Instead I drop my voice to a whisper. "Yes, of course I have."

"If you find the top, can you wear it on Saturday? It looks great with your pink pearls."

I end the call so he can't tell I'm crying. Even if I do find his favourite top, it no longer fits over my double D milk factories. But it would look fantastic on Agnes, along with the pearls.

Agnes is still in the kitchen; I can hear her slicing veg for dinner. Finn is asleep, but to put him down could break the spell so I hold his head above my heart, then I tiptoe upstairs to check my jewellery box.

Steven stands behind me as I brush my teeth. He throws something to the floor. "Bloody hell, Hannah, what's going on inside your head? These were at the bottom of the washing basket." White skinny jeans lie crookedly, like broken legs, beside my bare feet. I don't say anything. I'm naked wearing only a string of pink pearls. "You look exhausted," he continues more gently. "Are you getting enough rest during the day? You should use Agnes to do as much as possible." He pinches the flesh under my arm. "Are you eating enough? You're skin and bones. Christ, Hannah, you need to look after yourself better than this."

Using the back of my hand, I wipe toothpaste from my lips. "He never stops gorging. He's always hungry, Steven. Always at me." Tears plop into the porcelain sink. "He's a monster."

I expect his anger to deepen, but he strokes the back of my neck. "Hush, sweetheart. Tomorrow morning I'll make an appointment for you and Finn to see the Health Visitor. Perhaps, there's some sort of problem..."

He means with me. There's a problem with me.

Steven's fingers hesitate over my dove tattoo then linger on the warm pearls; he fumbles with the clasp and slips them off my neck.

"I don't think either of us is really in the mood tonight," he says.

Dr Pearson is called in to see me. The Health Visitor isn't happy with Finn's progress. He's not putting on weight despite the constant feeding and the situation can't be allowed to continue.

"How are you coping, Mrs Cavell?" Dr Pearson smiles like a boy. He barely looks older than Agnes.

I had promised myself I wouldn't cry, but he's not playing the game by opening with this question. Looking down at my lap, I shake my head.

"Clearly Finn is running you ragged. It's a vicious circle. He's constantly feeding because he's constantly hungry. You never recover so can't produce enough milk to satisfy him."

Steven and his mother are right. The problem is me.

Dr Pearson explains there is a solution and I feel an impulse to kiss his baby face. I could strip naked and let him take me right there in the surgery because he has *an answer*. An answer I could have worked out for myself if I hadn't been brainwashed by the post-natal police, Steven and his 'breast is best' mother.

Formula milk will allow me to cope and I can switch Finn immediately. This means somebody else can feed him, even during the night. I can rest, sleep and leave the house without him. My boobs can return to normal and I can start having sex with my husband again.

This time I'm crying with relief.

I wake at five 'o'clock, having slept through since ten the night before. Seven consecutive hours of sleep! Dr Pearson, along with the manufacturer of formula milk, is a miracle maker. Turning over, I stretch out for Steven, but the sheet is cold – he must be up already. I almost hold my breath listening out for Finn's cries, but hear nothing. The creak of the central heating system is the only indication that the house is stirring, preparing for the day ahead.

Steven is in the kitchen making coffee. I slip my arms around his waist, kiss his warm neck. His skin smells shower clean, feels smooth, he must have just shaved. "You're up early," I murmur and begin to nibble at his earlobe.

He looks at his watch. "Long day today – gotta wrap up that deal, remember? Lots of loose ends to tie up. You sound perky this morning."

I smile lazily. "I feel great. See, all I needed was a good night's sleep."

"And Finn?"

"What about Finn?"

Steven pulls away from me, pours coffee into his travel mug. "Have you checked on him?"

"Not yet." My good mood is already wilting. "It's all quiet upstairs so I assume he's still sleeping."

"But you didn't check?" Steven pulls on his jacket, tightens his tie. "He was crying in the night. Did you feed him?"

The tiles under my bare feet feel ice-cold. "No, I slept straight through. Agnes said she would make a bottle if he was hungry."

"So the au pair is now feeding my son?"

"That is one of the benefits of switching to formula," I say, keeping my voice calm.

His shoulders sag. "You're sticking with this then? Giving up on the breastfeeding for good."

"Finn is always hungry because I'm not producing enough milk. Dr Pearson was worried about Finn's weight – apparently he's dropped under the growth curve." I keep talking because Steven's eyes are staring into me. His jaw is clenched. "Lots of women stop breastfeeding a lot earlier than me, it's perfectly normal."

"Did Dr Pearson think your recent behaviour was *perfectly normal*? Did you tell him about your irrational thoughts, your weird suspicions about Agnes?"

I don't know how to reply. Steven had insisted, demanded, I visit the Health Centre to sort out Finn. Now he was angry with me again, even though I'd done what he'd asked.

Steven's face bounces back into a smile. I reach for his hand, but he's looking past me into the hallway. Agnes stands at the bottom of the stairs, Finn balanced on one hip gurgling happily. Her lemon silk robe is embroidered with crimson roses; I have one just like it. She holds out Steven's briefcase, saying without any trace of an accent, "Don't forget this."

I watch my husband stride towards the au pair. He doesn't kiss me goodbye or even look back. For one dreadful moment, I think he's going to kiss Agnes, but he leans down to Finn and kisses the top of our baby's head.

I often play a game with myself; imagine what Helen would be doing now if I'd been chosen for The Nutcracker. If I had died with Mum and Dad on the A27 that December afternoon and she'd stayed home, what sort of life would Helen be living in my place? I doubt her husband would hire an au pair behind her back. Nor would she meekly let a thieving, lying stranger usurp her position. Helen would look for proof and catch the bitch out.

Steven is getting the Champagne I forgot to pick up for tonight's dinner with his parents. He's taken Finn along, for once, and Agnes has joined them as she's booked an appointment with the beauty salon in the village. This means I'm alone in the house. Alone to explore Agnes' room.

I don't find a pair of white jeans in her wardrobe; neither do I find any of my missing things. The top drawer of her bedside cabinet is full of underwear. The other drawers are empty. So too is the antique dressing table, squatting like a Victorian cuckoo in the small room. Disappointingly, there is nothing belonging to me in Agnes's bedroom.

Having been deprived of sleep for so long, my body now seeks every opportunity to lie down and sink into oblivion. Pressing my face into the clean white pillows, I smell lavender. I smell long hot summer days when Helen and I splashed and giggled in our paddling pool. Dad would fill it on the patio using the leaky hosepipe from the garden tap. I can just lie down for a moment. Think through all the places Agnes could hide my pearls. Steven won't be back for hours.

When I wake, the room is dark. The day has slipped by. It

must be early evening. Nobody has come to find me.

In the hallway, I hear voices from the dining room. The clink of crystal. The lilting rise and fall of easy-going chatter between dinner guests. Steven's parents must be here already. Oddly, the kitchen is empty. The electric oven is humming and my stomach cramps at the aroma of roasting meat. Steven's probably showing off Agnes to his mother. *This is Hannah's replacement. She cooks and cleans and never drops Finn on his head. Isn't she wonderful?*

The dining room door swings open. Steven's mother carries dishes through to the kitchen with Steven in her wake. She's in full flow. "The au pair must be doing something right; Helen's looking absolutely marvellous. Such a clever decision of yours, darling, to get some help in."

Why did she call me Helen?

Steven sees me in the doorway. His eyes narrow, the relaxed smile vanishes. "Where the hell have you been, Agnes?" he says, pausing only to stack the pile of soup bowls he was holding on the draining board. "Helen's had to prepare everything herself."

They're both frowning at me. All I can do is stutter back, "W-what are you talking about? I'm Hannah."

Steven's mother wipes her hands on a tea towel. "Then why did you tell my son your name was Agnes?" She turns to Steven. "I told you to hire an English girl. Did you check her references?"

I have to see for myself.

In the dining room, Agnes sits at the head of the table with Finn on her lap. He's beaming like a Buddha, sucking on a breadstick. Her long hair has been cut into a slick short bob. She's wearing my cream top with diamante straps, a pink pearl necklace around her flushed neck.

"I can't believe what you've done to your hair," says Steven. He knocks my elbow as he strides past to stand behind Agnes. With palms pressed against her arms, he looks back at me. "First you steal Helen's clothes and now you cut off all your hair. This is beyond a joke."

He's shouting at me. Not at Agnes. At me.

The dove tattoo on Agnes's left shoulder is clearly visible in the round mirror behind her. Then I realise I'm looking at her reflection. The tattoo is actually on her right side – the opposite shoulder to mine.

The young woman in my seat stares at me. "Helen?" I whisper almost hopefully, calling out to the past. Her grey-blue eyes are unreadable. She doesn't smile or acknowledge me in any way.

Steven's mother joins in the shouting. Finn begins to cry. I step forward, to go to my son, but Steven's cold glare fixes me. Agnes whispers something to Finn. He drops the breadstick, whimpers and reaches for her neck.

I back out of the dining room and run to Agnes' bedroom where I trip over her rucksack.

I can cope with this, I chant inside my head. Like I coped with Helen's death. Coped without Mum and Dad.

I start packing clothes into the rucksack. Under a book on the bedside cabinet is a pile of cash – I grab it all. From the ensuite bathroom I take make-up and toiletries, even her toothbrush.

Downstairs, Steven and his parents are talking loudly. With my hand on the door latch, I feel a knot of pain in my breast, as if someone is squeezing inside, but my milk dried up days ago. Finn is no longer crying. My replacement is coping.

HOUSEHOLD GODS

Mohammed placed the cube of lamb into the ceramic dish, its minty aroma mingling with the hint of cranberry and cinnamon from the lighted candle. He'd bought a range of Christmas-spiced tea lights in the January sales, which would help to keep Vesta's flame alight. When he had to leave the house, Mo blew it out, not trusting Vesta's naked flame alone with his mother.

Into the second dish he poured a libation of elderflower cordial. "Accept my offerings, Janus, and help to ease the ending I face today," he whispered, eyes open and fixed on the homemade shrine. Typically he sought Vesta's blessing, as protector of the home and family, before leaving the house, but Mo felt that the sad and difficult day ahead required additional support. He repeated the request six more times under his breath.

Later he would bring cake for his household gods. He was a good son, but a poor Muslim, and had promised his mother he would bring home a cake: Victoria sponge, with real jam, her favourite, to celebrate the prophet's birthday. Today he would also visit the hospital to see the baby for the first, and possibly last, time; born on the first day of the year and now twenty-four days old. Not a day for celebrations.

Despite not eating meat since he was nine years old, the same age he'd discovered his true faith, Mo wrinkled his nose approvingly at the tempting smell of the minted lamb. After finishing his morning shift at Meadowbank garden centre, Mo had chopped and spoon-fed the rest of the steak, along with garlic mash and home grown petis pois, to Mummy. He liked to see her eat a good lunch before he set off for the library. Friday afternoons, his one afternoon off, were for study and the world wide web was his undisputed god of research. He didn't own a computer; at two o'clock each Friday he would take his place at one of the public terminals in the town's library."

The telephone call, coming as Mo helped his mother waddle back from the commode, had exploded his afternoon plans. Mo checked his pulse, ninety-eight and rising, but could not ignore the clipped vowels of the duty nurse who instructed him to come *immediately* and say goodbye to his daughter.

Extinguishing Vesta's flame, he bowed towards the shrine, eyes closed, to murmur a final prayer. He kept the shrine in his bedroom so as not to upset Mummy. Mo had created his design from photographs he'd found on the Internet of a typical Roman household shrine. The finished relief appeared authentic with its weathered (cold coffee worked a treat) columns and sloping roof chiselled from modelling plaster. First tracing with heavy pencil the dancing figures and the writhing snake, Mo later coloured in the sketches using a tin of watercolour paints he'd found in an attic crate of his old toys and books. Balanced on the apex of the shrine was a stone statue, with two faces, both adorned with long curling beards. The god Janus, protector of doors and gateways, was often represented by two heads to signify how he could simultaneously watch both the past and the future. Mo didn't envy the god this talent, he could barely think about the past, let alone face the future.

If Mo had made an offering to give thanks for the baby's birth, then maybe he wouldn't now have to make the torturous visit to her hospital incubator – to stand with Aisha and pretend to grieve for another man's child.

Mo selected a TV channel showing an afternoon of black and white films, tucked the blanket of crocheted squares around his mother's legs, and kissed her dry forehead.

"I have to go out, Mummy," he said clearly to her blank face, "I will ask Mrs Harris to pop in later and make you more tea. You like your afternoon tea, don't you, Mummy?"

She blinked, as if in acknowledgement, but her dark eyes looked past him. Pulling the curtains across to keep the heat in, Mo flicked the light switch on and off seven times before crossing the threshold. He quietly closed the door to his mother's sitting room and repeated the action with the kitchen, downstairs cloakroom and hall lights. The front door was safely chained and double-locked, so he let himself out through the kitchen door. He locked and unlocked the door six times and then, after a quick prayer invoking the blessing of Janus, he locked it one final time.

Mo dropped the key into Mrs Harris' shaking hand, being careful not to brush against her fingers.

"Yes, dear," she chirped, "I know how Mrs Khan likes her tea. I'll look in on her after the three o'clock at Chepstow. Now she won't need the loo or anything, will she?"

He shook his head. Mo was below average height, but he still looked down at his neighbour, the tight white curls of her perm hugging her scalp in the snapping easterly wind.

"She went after lunch," he said, starting to back away from the old lady.

"Oh, that's lovely, dear." There was a splash of lipstick on a lower tooth and the cherry-red hadn't made it all the way round her cracked lips. "Your mother is rather a big-boned lady."

With older women, particularly white English ladies, Mo always felt the need to end an interaction with a slight bow. He did this now to hide the twitch of a smile. He knew Mrs Khan's bones were no bigger than any other Pakistani woman of her age, but they were significantly well insulated.

Mrs Harris stretched out her arm, almost as if she were about to stroke his head, but then pulled it back to her chest. "God be with you," she whispered and then scuffled back inside her house.

Which god, thought Mo, *when there were so many to choose from?* Two days after his ninth birthday Mohammed had woken to find Uncle Osman, nicknamed Oz, squatting at the edge of his bed, tears rolling down his shiny cheeks. Usually he had the smiling appearance of a garden Buddha, but that night Uncle Oz sagged like a deflating rubber ring. He gurgled and spluttered and finally spat out a story involving a lorry, a moped and Mo's father's delivery van. There was no happy ending to the bedtime tale. Mo buried the details of his uncle's words and accepted that his father was gone. He had left them for good. Uncle Oz told Mo he had to pray to God, pray for his father. But what was the point of prayers for a dead man?

At nine years old, Mo had decided one god wasn't enough. If you were to protect and keep safe all those you loved, then you needed a whole battalion. Multiple prayers to multiple deities distributed your fielders across a dangerous pitch. At least one of them should always be there, in place to take that fateful catch. The Romans hedged all their bets by spreading their wishes and prayers across a multitude of gods. Mo adopted their beliefs because it was the perfect religious contingency, removing risk and misery from his fragile existence.

He also reasoned that his father, when leaving the safety and sanctuary of the family home, had left himself open to the fates. Crossing the threshold from inside to out was a dangerous undertaking. By his tenth birthday, Mo had developed numerous strategies to cope with the challenge of endless doorways.

Mo continued with his beliefs and little rituals that had begun after his father's death. However, according to Uncle Oz, a single man over thirty needed a wife. After Mummy's second, and more debilitating stroke, Mo could no longer cope with her alone and continue to work at the garden centre. Several carer visits were scheduled each day to help bathe and feed Mrs Khan while Mo was working. Uncle Oz reasoned a wife would be a more permanent solution – and cheaper.

Uncle Oz took care of all the arrangements and Aisha was shipped to Sussex. She came from a good family, known to his uncle, and brought with her one small suitcase of clothes. Mo's new wife spoke no English and, after five months, living in the provincial suburbs, had made little progress with her vocabulary. With Uncle Oz she'd spoken only Urdu. To Mo she said little more than, "Good morning, husband" and "Good night, husband," recited and learned from Uncle Oz. After the wedding, Mo moved to the spare bedroom and painted Aisha's room a pale lemon, a colour chosen to complement her favourite sari.

Mo always made an effort to tell his mother about his day at Meadowbank nursery. Talking to her was excellent therapy, or so he'd been told. She did not respond.

One evening, after an unexpected late shift at Meadowbank, Mo arrived home to find Aisha sitting with his mother. He watched the two women from beyond the kitchen door as Aisha spoon-fed his mother from a bowl of soup, chatting happily away in Urdu about her life before England. Aisha talked of her younger brothers and sisters and their silly pranks. She was funny. Her eyes were bright, her smile relaxed. Her long ebony hair, usually tightly pinned in a coil at the back of her head, hung loose across both shoulders. Mo crept up to his bedroom, leaving his wife undisturbed by his return.

Now Aisha was at the hospital, where she visited every day since the birth. Mo would be a dutiful husband and take his place at her side.

After reversing the car from the garage, Mo parked on the drive and returned to the house. He tugged on the front door and then the kitchen door; they were both secure. Finally murmuring some words of thanks to Vesta, he climbed back into the grey hatchback.

*

Mo spoke his name clearly into the box on the wall. A buzzer trilled and the glass-fronted door clicked open. Inside the Special Care Unit, a middle-aged nurse, wearing pristine white, escorted him to a corner room suffused with light. Winding an elastic band in her fingers, the nurse pulled her blonde hair into a ponytail, instantly making her look ten years younger. Turning on her heels, the ponytail almost slapping his face, the nurse strode off again, leaving Mo alone outside the door.

Mo peered through the round window, unsure if he could enter without an escort. Six incubators sat inside like elevated greenhouse trays. Three of them were watched over by electronic displays and hushed couples. By the fourth sat Aisha, her hands held in the lap of her sari, her head bowed.

"Mr Khan?" A loud, female voice came from behind him. Another nurse, this one wore a navy-blue uniform, squinted at him with dark, narrow eyes.

"Yes," he answered, backing up against the door, "but please call me Mo."

"Your English is excellent, Mr Khan. I'm surprised because your wife can hardly speak a word. Thankfully, one of the ward porters speaks Urdu and he's translated anything we needed to know from her." Her tone was scolding.

Mo wanted to counter, gently state he was as English as the next man, born in Brighton General and living in Sussex all his life, but the next man, jogging past in a flapping white coat, called out with an antipodean accent for someone to hold the main door. Instead, Mo replied, "My wife has only lived here for a short time."

One silver-grey eyebrow twitched as the older nurse sucked on her lip. "Your wife's vigil, Mr Khan, has been lonely. But you're here now and your company will ease the waiting."

He followed the blue nurse into the incubator room. The rhythmic sigh of oxygen pumps and the infrequent beep of some machine were the only background sounds. Aisha stood as her husband approached. Her gaze flicked from him to settle again on the baby lying beneath a Perspex roof.

The nurse spoke behind him. "A prem baby is particularly susceptible to infections, Mr Khan, we've treated the pneumonia as best we can but now it's—"

"—In the lap of the gods?" said Mo quietly.

"Simply down to the strength of your daughter's immune system," she finished.

He didn't see her leave, but the starched blue nurse was replaced by the smiling nurse in white, who stood so close Mo could smell antiseptic and cigarette smoke on her skin. She squeezed his hand.

In the men's toilets, Mo lathered his hands and wrists with soap, then rinsed them in the tepid water. Five times would be sufficient, he thought, but returned to the sink to wash twice more.

Walking back to the incubator room, Mo passed the open kitchen area where the navy-blue nurse stood, her back towards him, talking with a male colleague. "Poor mare, shipped over here and nobody cares enough to give her the tools to survive." Her voice carried above the stirring teaspoon of her colleague. "Told Jamal she was in love, that she had a boyfriend back in Pakistan — a medical student. But his family didn't approve or something and she was the one that had to leave. I feel sorry for her, dumped with a bloke she's never met and expected to start spitting out babies like chapattis."

The male nurse inclined his head towards Mo and the woman slowly twisted round to stare at him. She sipped at the mug in her hands, but didn't offer an apology.

He could leave now; drive home and get on with dinner. Mummy needed to eat before the temporary carer arrived to bathe her before bedtime. His duty at the hospital had been executed, he'd seen the baby as requested – what more was there for him to do? Aisha wasn't going anywhere, so his presence was irrelevant.

The smiling nurse held open the door to the incubator room and gestured to Mo, "Are you coming back in, Mo?"

A strand of hair had slipped free to dangle across her cheek. Mo needed to see her push it back into place, but she kept the door open with her backside unaware of her unbalanced hair.

"No," he said, deciding quickly, "not yet."

Something flashed in her blue eyes, like the reflected glint of a flame. She was beautiful, Mo realised, quite beautiful. "A child is always a blessing," she said. A frown creased her forehead, yet the words were tender and soothed him.

Beyond the sliding doors of the main reception, Mo turned his mobile back on. A man in a striped dressing gown leant against a pillar, taking long drags from a cigarette; his other hand supported the stand of his drip with the tube still attached, disappearing up his sleeve. The sky looked tired, drained of light. Clouds hung low, grey and brooding, swollen with the promise of snow.

The baby was another man's child. Mo was certain on the paternity of Aisha's daughter because of two things. Firstly, his new wife had landed at Heathrow already three months pregnant – Uncle Oz confessed this before her arrival – and secondly, he had never slept in her bed. Mo lost his virginity during his teenage bacchanalian phase, a time of experimentation and too much vodka. Alison, with hair the colour of copper piping, let him *do it* at the end of school party in her parent's room.

He was sixteen and had already starting working at the garden centre. There were, occasionally, other girls after Alison but Mo had not yet consummated his marriage with Aisha. She was a stranger to him. After Mummy's first stroke, his affliction had worsened to the point where Mo could barely tolerate the touch of another human being.

The man with the drip raised his eyebrows and nodded, tossing Mo a silent *alright mate*. Mo turned away to stare across the car park where an ambulance was backing towards the doors of A and E.

"Mrs Harris?" he spoke into his mobile. He turned up the volume to hear the old lady's whispery voice. "Oh, good, I'm glad Mrs Khan enjoyed her afternoon tea. Could I possibly ask another favour, Mrs Harris?" Snow was falling now. "Yes, I will be here for some hours. If you could sit with..." Drip man stubbed his cigarette against the concrete pillar and let it fall. Specks of snow began to settle on the tarmac. "Mummy, Mrs Khan, loves soup – thank you. Yes, I will let my wife know you are praying for our daughter."

A child is always a blessing.

Mo shut down the phone. How did Mrs Harris know the baby was a girl? He'd never talked about Aisha's baby with Mrs Harris. Had Aisha learned more English than he realised?

His right hand was shaking. Mo hadn't changed out of his work clothes, so still wore the green uniform of the garden centre: drill trousers, polo shirt, sweatshirt and the ivy-green fleece with Meadowbank's red and gold logo. It was the cold of course; he was bound to shiver, standing inert outside in a snowstorm. As the doors slid open, Mo saw himself in the glass, a short brown man in shabby green. His father had been lost for twenty-five years, but was now returned to them. Mo saw him all the time, whenever he faced his own reflection. The same receding hairline, the swelling bald spot racing to meet his forehead, and the same fearful eyes were all part of the inheritance. He held a finger under his nose. All he needed was a neatly-trimmed moustache and his father would be fully resurrected.

Did Janus watch over sliding doors? As the god of doorways he must lurk nearby, never dropping his guard no matter who entered.

Drip man shuffled past. "The gods walk amongst us," said the man, staring straight ahead. From the back, his thick neck bulged, prickled with stubble, almost like a second chin.

"Excuse me, what did you say?"

The man stopped, turning to blink at Mo. "Sorry, mate, didn't say nothing."

"My mistake," said Mo.

Aisha had been crying. A paper towel lay scrunched in her lap and dark lines creased her eyelids. The incubator was open and for the first time, Mo peered into the baby's self-contained world. A nappy hung off the baby's bony hips. From her nose, protruded a plastic tube, taped across her tummy. She wore one pink, hand-knitted mitten, on her right hand. The other was bare and the fingers twitched in time with the rise and fall of her chest.

"You can hold her hand if you wish." The nurse in white was once again at Mo's side. He glanced at her and she nodded. "There's little she can catch from you that will do any more harm than pneumococcus."

Before he could prepare himself, the baby's hand curled around his finger. Her grip was surprisingly strong. His breathing raced to match his heartbeat, but he was determined not to pull away from her touch. Mo gazed at the creases on her coffee skin; the baby's hand looked like his own, a perfect replica, but in miniature.

"Why is she wearing a mitten?" said Mo.

"To stop her pulling out the tube. Aisha expresses her milk and we feed baby through the tube, it goes straight into her stomach. She is a bit small, and weak, to feed by mouth."

"But why only one mitten?"

Her expression softened. "Somehow she lost the other one before you came in. We can't find it anywhere."

Mo recalled the telephone message he'd picked up earlier. The navy-blue nurse was called Janet, now he remembered. "Janet told me she may not last the night, that she is very weak."

"So many of them try to grow wings, but I believe your little girl wants to stay. Do you have a name for her?"

Would a name anchor her? Weigh down her wings? A nagging voice whispered inside his head, his mother's voice. She cannot meet God without a name.

Another voice spoke to him, Aisha's quiet voice. "Nadira."

"Nadira, after my mother?"

Aisha nodded.

"This baby is a rare and precious gift; let her bring love into your home." The nurse's words unfurled around them like an embrace. Mo looked away from Aisha, but the pony-tailed woman had already slipped away. Mo didn't know the nurse's name, as she hadn't worn a nametag. She didn't return to say goodbye at the end of her shift and he never saw her again in the unit.

"You've been very helpful to Mummy," Mo said in Urdu to Aisha.

"I wish I'd known her before the stroke. I think we would have become friends."

Mo hesitated, swallowing several times. "I think she likes you very much." He thought of how Aisha read to her every day, of how she fed Mummy, waiting patiently for each mouthful to go down before gently offering another.

A hint of a smile crept onto Aisha's face. Her black eyes met his briefly then swept back to the baby. She wasn't conventionally pretty, her face a little too thin and pointed, but her eyes were kind. "I think she has a good son," said Aisha softly. "A kind and loving son."

He thought of what he'd overheard outside the nurse's kitchen. "You don't have to stay. You could go home... after." Mo stopped. There were no appropriate words to frame his meaning.

Aisha shook her head and replied carefully in English. "I want to stay." She reached forward to stroke her baby's chest and began to talk again in Urdu. "This is our home now. We will stay if you wish us to. I will ask nothing more of you."

Together they stood beside the incubator, watching over Nadira.

Snowflakes funnelled towards the windows like desperate white moths. The ticking machines and wheezing babies settled to a low, constant hum, as Mo began to recite his prayer. He didn't care which of the gods heard it – he knew they were all listening. Nadira snuffled like a kitten in her incubator, pawing at the feeding tube with her mittened hand, still tightly holding onto Mo's finger with the other.

At dawn, Mo drove Aisha home. Overnight, the snow had blown away and the roads were clear. They both planned to bathe and eat, before returning to the hospital to continue the vigil at their daughter's side. The budding wings had faded with the snow as the antibiotics finally kicked in. Baby Nadira was staying for now.

Mummy was lying on her back and a rattling snore told Mo she was still sleeping. Mrs Harris had spent the night, squashing in beside Mrs Khan to teeter at the edge of the counterpane. The old lady was also asleep; the white curls around her ear were stuck flat against the pillow and her face.

He returned to his own bedroom. It was time to give thanks to the household gods.

Someone had beaten him to it. Vesta's flame was alive and flickering before Mo's plaster shrine. He had extinguished the candle, and checked it seven times before leaving for the hospital, but now the candle was burning in its dish. Beside it lay a single pink woollen mitten.

A CINNAMON KISS

The bell above the door rang out, announcing Eliza's arrival at the bakery. Two friends followed her in, giggling and tossing glances towards Tobias. The girls all worked together in the milliner's shop at the posh end of the high street. Eliza's eyes closed and her cherry lips slid into a contented smile. Tobias hoped she was savouring the warmth of the shop, mingled with the tempting aroma of bitter hot chocolate and caramel, bubbling in their pots.

"The usual, Eliza?" said Tobias.

She nodded, then took off her bonnet, letting her golden curls bounce free. The three girls stopped by the bakery every morning, to sit at the table in the window, where Eliza demurely sipped her cup of chocolate. After placing a coin on the counter, Eliza asked, "Do you have something for me to try today, Toni?"

He whipped out a floral plate, topped with a delicate pastry shaped into an E. It was iced in pink and gold, sprinkled with almonds, which he knew were her favourites. She dipped her finger in the icing, then licked it clean. "Divine," she said, clapping her hands. "Toni, you are so clever. And for my friends?"

Tobias tipped two chocolate-dipped eclairs, oozing cream, along with a cluster of tiny macarons, as brightly coloured as jewels, into a box for her.

"Thank you," she gushed. "Could you bring them over to our table with my chocolate?"

When Eliza re-joined her friends, their three blonde heads bowed together in a shared joke, each one taking a turn to snatch a glance at the baker.

"One morning that snooty mare will remember your name," said Sally, Tobias's elder sister, nudging him with her floury elbow. She began unloading her tray of fruit tarts onto the counter shelves, huffing and puffing as she worked. "Then maybe you can start charging for those pastries. That girl is eating all our profits."

Once Eliza and her friends had left, Tobias set about clearing the table and sweeping up the flakes and crumbs they had shed like pastry snow across the tiled floor. The bell tinkled again. Jethro, the blacksmith's son, arrived to collect his father's lunch order. Tilly the terrier trotted at his heels, her claws clicking like clockwork. The blacksmith's appetite matched his girth: two dinner-plate sized pork pies, half a dozen scotch eggs and a slab of gingerbread.

Tilly sat back, berry-black snout pointing up at Tobias. He slid a chipolata from his apron pocket and into the terrier's open mouth. She swallowed the sausage in one gulp. "Just this once," said Tobias, ruffling her ears.

"Me and the lads are taking the dogs out tomorrow morning," said Jethro. "Going to catch ourselves a fat hare or two. Fancy joining us?"

Tobias couldn't think of anything more hateful than hare coursing. He shook his head. "Sorry, mate, but I need to fire up the ovens. Bakers work similar hours to hares you see, up before dawn and still going when the moon has risen."

Jethro shrugged his shoulders. "Then we'll see you in *The King's Head* at the end of the day. You can toast our success." He twisted round to wink at Sally. "That's unless you've got a date? Gone and asked her yet?"

"I don't know who you mean," said Tobias, staring at his boots.

Jethro slapped him on the back, then whistled for Tilly, the little dog skidding on the polished floor in her haste to keep up.

From behind the counter, Sally let out a loud, and not very lady-like, snort.

On the way to *The King's Head* for his evening pint, Tobias took a detour through the churchyard to visit Mum and Dad. Sally's boots were missing from the back steps of the bakery when he left, but he hadn't noticed his sister slipping out for the evening. She was probably tucked up in bed and had simply taken her boots inside to clean.

The edge of the moon had been sliced off, as if some giant creature had taken a bite. In two nights' time, it would be full and round. His parents' grave nestled beside the boundary hedge; they slept together in death as they had lain together in their marital bed for almost thirty years. Tobias slumped onto the cold grass, his heavy head aching with thoughts of Eliza. Even with his eyes shut, he still saw her pretty face, heard her honey voice. She was his true love, he was certain, but how could he win that precious first kiss from her?

A snuffling sound snapped open his eyes. There was movement behind the lichen-speckled tomb of a long dead merchant. Tobias realised he wasn't alone. It was a hare. He tugged his supper from his pocket, an unsold cinnamon bun, and began to tear it apart. Tobias tossed a handful of crumbs towards the hare. The animal did not flinch, and to his surprise stretched out to eat the scraps. She was the most beautiful creature he had ever seen. The hare was small compared to the large bucks he saw leaping through the meadow. It had to be a doe.

He threw more of the bun and the hare ate up every morsel, edging closer. Scattering the last crumbs onto his hand, he held it out with his palm flat. He held his breath as the hare blew warm air across his fingertips. Her whiskers tickled; they were speckled with white flecks, like the flour dust at the bakery.

Tobias feared scaring her but he had to warn the hare. He kept his voice low. "The lads are hunting tomorrow at dawn, taking the dogs to the fields. Please keep close to the church. Hide out here and stay safe."

How stupid was he, talking to a hare? Yet, she crouched beside him as if listening to his words. Only when the church clock began to chime the hour did she stir, springing up and twisting gracefully in the air. Before he could blink, the hare had gone.

The following evening, Tobias drank down his tankard and left *The King's Head* early to head back to the churchyard. He had to know if the hare was safe. On his way out, he slunk past Jethro, trying to sell a pair of limp, lifeless rabbits to the landlord.

The moon glowed high above the church tower. This time he'd brought two cinnamon buns, snatched fresh from the kitchen. He laid a crumb trail all the way to his parents' grave, sat by the simple wooden cross and waited.

When at last the hare appeared, his legs and backside were numb, his bare hands stiff and frozen. She came right up to his outstretched hand, yet ignored the chunks of bun he held.

The hare sat onto her haunches; her liquorice black eyes stared into him. "Thank you," she said.

Tobias shook his head. The hare was talking to him. He'd had one tankard of beer. One only. Perhaps downed it too fast?

"Your warning saved my life. For that, I can grant you a wish. Tell me what your heart desires."

Oddly, her voice sounded familiar. Strange magic, thought Tobias with a shiver. She must be an enchanted creature — a pretty young woman cursed by a witch and trapped inside a hare's body. His mum had told him such tales when they worked in the bakery, kneading and preparing the dough, while his sister Sally had always scoffed at such nonsense.

The hare considered one paw carefully, licking between her toes. "Your legs are long, your shoulders broad, Tobias — you would make a handsome hare." She stroked her paw along the silken edge of one ear. "How can I repay your kindness?"

Tobias swallowed hard, coughing to clear his throat, then asked, "Please help me win my true love's kiss. Her name is Eliza Stoneheart."

The hare paused in her grooming. "The mason's daughter? Are you quite sure about that?"

How could she know these things about the townsfolk? And for that matter, how had she known *his* name? The hare must have lived amongst them, once upon a time.

"I love Eliza," he said, "but she barely knows I exist."

The magical hare proceeded to recite a special recipe. It was guaranteed to win Tobias his true love's kiss. Before finishing, the hare beckoned him close so she could whisper the final secret ingredient.

Tobias rocked back onto his heels, frowning. "That's hardly a secret ingredient for a baker."

She wrinkled her nose and spoke sharply, "It must remain a secret to Eliza. Only then will your wish be granted. Do you understand, Tobias?"

Bowing his head, he nodded, yet doubted her instructions. When he looked up to ask another question, the hare had vanished. From the woodlands beyond the churchyard came the bark of a fox. She must have caught its scent and fled.

What the hare had described was a simple pastry with commonplace flavours. But then Eliza adored sweet pastries, and perhaps the wise hare knew this. He would return to the bakery, work all through the night to be ready for Eliza's daily visit. Tobias stopped mid-stride, trailing his hand through his hair. Was this trickery? No, surely it was no more than a secret recipe. A shortcut to love. One taste and Eliza would toss back her curls, lean in with soft lips to deliver true love's kiss. With that thought, he gobbled down the remaining bun, relishing the best bit: the cinnamon-infused icing.

The next night, when Tobias finally trudged through the churchyard, the path brightly lit by the fat full moon, the hare was waiting, her languid limbs stretched out across his parents' grave. He threw down a paper bag and the pastries tumbled out before her like an offering. The hare edged forwards, to sniff and then nibble on the nearest one.

"Oh Tobias," she said, sprinkling flakes across her fur, "these are delicious. You baked the recipe perfectly."

He crumpled to the ground to sit cross-legged beside the hare, his head in his hands as he cried, "Your recipe didn't work! They were supposed to win me my true love's kiss, but Eliza hated them."

"Perhaps Eliza is not your true love," said the hare.

Everybody else who visited the bakery that morning had adored the pastries, he told her. The news of Tobias' fabulous cinnamon kisses soon spread throughout the village. The Mayor sent for two boxes and ordered a daily delivery to his chambers. Even the blacksmith arrived in person, Jethro and Tilly skulking behind him, to sample the delicious new treat that everyone was talking about. He took a dozen back to the forge, cancelling his usual gingerbread pudding.

When Tobias delivered the special pastry reserved for Eliza, she had gasped in surprise. Each pastry had been twisted into an X, a kiss, and for Eliza's he had wound around it a pastry heart decorated with vermillion icing and chopped almonds.

Raising the pastry heart to her lips, she said excitedly, "I can smell rosewater and vanilla."

Tobias awaited the moment he had long dreamt of. Eliza would kiss him fervently, declaring how she felt the same, that she loved him too.

"Ugh!" Eliza ripped the pastry heart apart, throwing one half at him. "My lips are tingling. What did you put in this?" She turned to her two friends, shouting, "Is my face swelling?"

Tobias watched in horror as his dream shattered. "I call them cinnamon kisses. I baked them especially for you, Eliza," he said in desperation.

"I loathe and despise cinnamon." She patted her cheeks, then studied the backs of her hands. "Look! I'm coming out in lumps already. Soon I will be a mass of pimples. You've done this to me. I hate you!"

While Tobias recounted the events of that morning, the hare continued to feast on the pastry kisses.

"Oh dear, poor Tobias," said the hare, her whiskers twinkling with icing sugar. "But how could a baker's wife not love cinnamon? Eliza could never be the one for you."

He stuffed half a pastry into his mouth. The cinnamon perfectly complimented the stickiness, enhancing the more subtle flavouring of rosewater. He had to agree with the hare: if Eliza didn't love cinnamon then she couldn't be his true love. But then what was to become of him?

The hare crept closer, pushing her velvet nose to rest against his cheek. She smelled of meadow-sweet hay, of dawn dew and the first snap of a winter morning's frost. Suddenly, the idea came to him. It was obvious. He would kiss the hare and break her enchantment. She would return to her true form, become once again the beautiful young woman trapped inside.

Before Tobias could act, the hare pressed her mouth onto his. He tasted wet grass and bitter, gritty soil. The hare pulled away with a loud snort, unchanged.

Tobias hunched forwards onto all fours. The tombs and gravestones became towers as he shrank towards the dank earth. With his head back, he felt his ears growing, long and silky, over the curve of his spine. His limbs were taut and muscular, ready to flee at the slightest sound.

He could no longer smell the hare. In the gloom, a new shape stretched towards the sky like a tree. A pink round moon peered down, a human face. His nostrils clogged with the stink of stale yeast and lard.

A scolding voice made his ears throb, Sally's voice. "If you had *actually* bothered listening to Eliza you'd know how much she hated cinnamon. All you saw was her pretty face, such a stupid boy. True love," his sister said, her voice mocking, "there's no such thing. Serves you right for trying to ensnare her with a love spell." She flicked his sensitive nose. "Now I get the bakery all to myself and I certainly won't be giving away the profits."

Thoughts jumbled together in the remains of his memory. Sally, his own sister, had bewitched him. When he believed her early to bed on moonlit nights, she'd been roaming the countryside as a hare.

Another scent engulfed him, a foul and fetid stench: *dog*.

"Can you smell that, brother? Jethro and his mangy terrier, the one you fed with our best sausages. I doubt Tilly will recognise you tonight." Tobias felt rough hands around his long ears, wrenching him into the air. Sally's laugh rang out. "Jethro's always punctual and I've promised my lover his favourite dish tonight: jugged hare."

As he swung upwards in his sister's firm grip, he glimpsed his new reflection in a puddle. His final human thought was how Sally had been right about one thing: he did indeed make a handsome hare.

A GOOD WORD

The young woman was in the office hut, where the computers squatted like fat hens on the central desk. He watched through the grubby Perspex of the door as she bent towards some papers. A silver chain glinted against her neck, the crucifix suspended in the air above the swell of her breasts pushing out a plain white T-shirt. She looked up and waved him in.

"What do you want?" She arched backwards, hands on her waist. He felt like a skinny stray dog cowering before her, but he had orders and couldn't slink away.

"Ma'am," he began, but faltered, looking down at his scuffed boots. A smear of rust, or blood, marked his left toecap. "I was told to collect papers for the general, ma'am."

"I don't bite." She parted her lips to show small, even teeth. "Well, not without good cause." Wiping a trickle of sweat from her cheek, she held out a cardboard folder. She didn't offer her name, but he knew it was Esther. Her skin was much lighter than his. He'd heard talk in the compound that her father was English, white and rich. "These are the stats he wants. You'd better get them to him quickly."

"Stats?"

"Statistics. Figures." Esther sighed a little. "The numbers your general needs." Her round eyes widened, making him fidget with the strap of his rifle. "He asked for data on his little mountain troop. I've collated several reports so he has the full picture."

"They say you went to school in England?" He pushed the rifle back over his shoulder, trying to match her proud stare. She spoke in Swahili but some of her long words buzzed inside his head like flies.

"I was born there, grew up in Brighton. Do you know where that is?"

He shook his head, but couldn't stop grinning. This girl was talking to him as if he knew stuff.

Esther's lips twitched, softening. "It's a big town in the south of England, beside the sea."

"Tell me about the sea. What does it taste like?"

With his breath fogging before him, Gideon struggled to remember the heat of the mountain forests. The woollen gloves kept his fingers from trembling as he pulled up the remaining tomato plants. Esther always boasted how the English weather brought a new surprise each day. Air that froze your words or the numbing easterly wind that made your ears ache, these were surprises he could do without. The rain in the Congo was warm, life-giving. Sussex rain seeped into your bones, making you forget the sun ever existed.

Mo was struggling to untie the knots binding the tomato stems to the bamboo canes. The string had hardened into brittle unworkable clumps. If Mo removed the stiff gardening gloves, then he'd have a chance of working the knots free with bare hands, but Gideon knew this would never happen.

Gideon took the shiny red penknife from his pocket. "Let me help," he said. He began to cut through the knots, the maze of twisted stems slumped to the earth like a line of men dropping in front of a firing squad. Mo slid out the canes, one by one, and laid them neatly beside the sprouting rows of winter veg. The turnips were Mo's idea; they fed the soil with nitrogen and other nutrients so it would be fertile, ready for planting in the spring. Mo worked at a garden centre, so Gideon listened and tried to learn from him. Whenever he had a free shift from the care home, he helped out with Mo's allotment. During the summer, he had stopped by every day to water the tomatoes, two pints per plant as Mo instructed, when the plants were in full bloom. He had nothing to offer for the running costs, but Mo never asked and always split the harvest fifty-fifty.

"I love hearing how you met Esther," said Mo, standing upright. "But what was all that about tasting the sea?" His laugh was quiet and contained.

"I had never seen the sea." Gideon looked down to the sliver of sock poking through the hole in his trainers. "Her eyes were so wide and round. I was a foolish boy."

Mo pinched off the still green tomatoes and tossed them along with the fallen fruit into a black bucket. "Maybe Aisha can use these to make chutney." For once, Gideon was thankful to be spared his share of the crop – he would only throw them away. "I guess the Democratic Republic of Congo is landlocked," Mo continued, as if thinking aloud. "But still, Esther must have thought you were nuts or something. How did you get her to go out with you?"

"All the rangers fancied her." Gideon folded his arms, thinking of the salty tang of Esther's lips. "But she chose me."

"Yeah, it must have been your boyish charm," said Mo with another laugh.

The grey clouds sagged above them, almost low enough to touch. Near the boundary fence, a lone man worked beside a shed. Earlier he had stood, hands in pockets, looking back, watching them. Mo called out to him, "How's it going?" The man kept on with his digging, didn't look round.

"I don't remember seeing him before." Gideon sucked in a breath; it stung his throat – the air was cooling fast as the light slipped away.

"That's Keith. He's taken over old Mr Parker's plot."

The digging man stood up for a moment and pulled off his hat to reveal a shaven head. He was as tall as the shed, but broad with a thick, short neck. He didn't call back, but seemed to stare at Gideon.

"What happened to Mr Parker?" Gideon pulled on the fur-lined hood of his anorak, so the man disappeared from view.

"He died back in the spring. Don't you remember me telling you?"

Gideon shrugged. He couldn't remember every death.

Walking back to where Mo had parked on the street, they had to pass the digging man. Tucking both hands into his anorak, Gideon fixed his eyes on the path. Mo called out a "good-night" without any response from Keith.

The street-lamps were coming on, glowing a feeble orange in the half-light. Mo stopped beside a silver Peugeot. "Can I give you a lift?"

Gideon handed back the bucket. He peered into the car. No crumpled papers, cartons or wrappers on the floor. The driver's seat was protected with a plastic sheet as if the car were brand new. The gesture of a lift was Mo's equivalent of pulling off his gardening glove and offering his hand. Shaking his head, he saw how quickly Mo relaxed. His shift at the care home started soon, but it wasn't far and Gideon liked to walk.

Mo lifted the bucket into the boot of his car. "You talked about a general earlier. Were you a soldier?"

"That was our nickname for the chief ranger; he loved barking out orders," Gideon answered without hesitation, then asked, "How is the baby? You didn't mention her today."

Mo brought out his mobile and flicked through the photo album. He swivelled it sideways so the image filled the screen. "She's crawling now."

Aisha, Mo's wife, knelt ahead of the baby, her face narrow and sharp, though her eyes shone. Gideon liked that. She reminded him of Esther with their daughter, Blessing, at that age. Blessing had been born in the back of a bullet-riddled truck crossing the border into Uganda. He retrieved a square paper photo from his wallet. Fingering over the creases, he held it alongside Mo's mobile. "My two angels," he said. With his other hand, he felt for the crucifix on its silver chain around his neck.

"Do you have any recent photos? Blessing must be growing up fast."

"No." He kissed the slim woman in the photograph, then the little girl balanced on her hip, and tucked them back into his wallet. Gideon sighed.

"Don't be too hard on yourself. You and Esther seem to work all hours. There can't be much time to spend together as a family."

Arriving in England, he'd chosen Worthing, along the coast from where Esther had been born, for their new home. The town's library offered free Internet access. On his first visit, Gideon met a skinny little man ("call me Mo") who shyly coached him in the rules, there were many, for using the library computers. Mo left his terminal frequently to visit the toilets on the first floor. Once, Gideon had walked in to find Mo drying his hands with paper tissues. Mo returned to the sink and washed again with soap, coating his skin in a white froth. Gideon had to keep twisting round at the urinal, fascinated as Mo repeated the cycle at least four more times.

In England, Gideon kept his scalp smooth with yellow plastic razors. In the forest camp, he had a knife, the blade singing sharp. Shaving his head made him feel clean, kept him strong. This kept him alive. He wondered how Mo would have coped without paper towels and hot water on tap. But then staying clean in the jungle would have been the least of Mo's fears.

The Internet taught Gideon how the Congo mountain gorillas were primates of the genus *Gorilla*, species *G. beringei*. He memorized the Latin names, repeating them and other facts in his head as he walked to work. They sounded impressive when he told Mo about the role of park-rangers in the Virunga Mountains. "There are only seven hundred mountain gorillas left in the wild," he once recounted sadly, keeping his voice to a whisper just like Sir David Attenborough in the BBC documentary.

Mo often spoke of how Gideon's role in protecting the gorillas had been important work. "I read that many wardens and rangers were killed during the civil wars – dangerous work."

Several weeks after their first meeting in the library, Mo shared that there were vacancies at the garden centre where he worked. He offered to put in a good word. Gideon had longed to ask which word could be good enough, but he quickly turned Mo down, explaining how he had already started a job. The shifts at the care home were long but he was paid in cash each week. He didn't mind working nights, he was used to being on watch. Besides, he rarely slept, and when he did, he returned to Africa. He did not wish to go back there, not even in his dreams.

Mo was silent. Gideon guessed that the other man must have asked a question. Something about Esther and the care home perhaps? "Yes," he said confidently, "I rarely see her in the daylight." He gave a laugh.

The November air tasted of ash and smoke, sticking to the back of his throat like tar. Mo had parked opposite the recreation ground where a heap of junk had been layered with wooden planks pointing towards the sky. A suit of clothes, stuffed with paper so it looked like a body, crowned the pyramid-shaped bonfire.

"Do you smell burning?" he said aloud. "Have they started the bonfire?"

"No, it won't be lit till Saturday evening. I can't smell anything." Mo went to close the boot lid but hesitated. "Almost forgot." He smiled weakly, his eyes flicking from Gideon to a supermarket bag beside the bucket. "Aisha thought this was a bit big for the baby." Mo passed him the bag. "I wondered if Blessing would like it," Mo swallowed, his voice fading as Gideon took out the toy. It was a furry black gorilla with a banana attached by Velcro to its leathery hand. "Not quite the same as the Silverbacks you're used to, but I thought it might bring back some happy memories."

Gideon knew he should laugh, reassure Mo that he got the joke, that he understood the nod to his park-ranger past. He held the cuddly toy in silence.

"I'm sorry," said Mo. "Blessing's far too old for such a thing. You don't have to take it..."

Since that day when the trucks arrived at his village, when he left his mama and sisters, nobody had freely given him anything without demanding something in return. Esther would scold him for being ungrateful. Mama would have pinched his ears and sent him back to say the magic words. Gideon straightened and the anorak hood fell back from his face. "Thank you," he said.

The third floor flat stank of charred meat. Gideon thought he would get used to it, but the smell grew worse each morning he returned from the night shift. There was a bathroom, complete with its own toilet, and one main room to cook, eat and sleep in. The whole flat was still bigger than the hut he'd shared in the village with Mama and his two younger sisters.

Three white plastic chairs were arranged in a semi-circle to face the small flat screen TV mounted on a cardboard box. He had bought it cheap from his Polish neighbours, two girls who worked in a hotel along the seafront. Kicking off his trainers, he sat in one of the chairs, propped the toy gorilla in another and stretched his legs across the third. He closed his eyes.

When he was still a boy of fifteen, four years before meeting Esther, a man came alone to his camp. In French, the man demanded to see the general, speaking proudly of the valuable gift he'd brought to honour the brave soldiers fighting for liberty. The man was a poacher. From his sack tumbled a pair of hands and a head, which rolled to settle at the general's boots. The limbs had been hacked from the body of a male gorilla, a Silverback, or so Gideon assumed from the distinctive domed head. The general picked up the creature's head, staring into its black eyes. Then, holding the head above his own, he lectured the camp on the economics of survival. Gideon remembered little of the speech other than the importance of the mountain gorillas to the tourist trade. The general had been a park-ranger before the war. The next morning, the poacher was propped naked against a single iroko tree at the edge of the camp. The gnarled and twisted tree gave good shade beside the track that led to the mountain road. The poacher's head and hands had been replaced with those of the gorilla, the huge hands sewn onto his wrists. Gideon's commander gave him the task of burning the blood-soaked sack and its contents.

He must have slept for an hour or so when Blessing climbed onto his lap, wrapping arms around his neck. "*Bon matin*, Papa." Her childish voice sang out, fully waking him. The braids of her plaited hair clung tight against her scalp; the smoky smell tainted them like the rest of the flat.

"No French," he said, then regretted his sharpness. "You must speak English now."

He felt something slap the back of his head. "Be nice to your daughter, Chidi," said Esther in Swahili. Then she kissed his cheek.

"You too!" Gideon couldn't help laughing at his beautiful girls. "And here my name is Gideon."

She flicked him again. "In our home, I will call you whatever I wish."

He grinned at her. "Truly, God has brought us safely home." Pushing off the cuddly toy, he tugged her down into the chair beside him. "Why me? All those men promising loyalty to your father and you picked me!"

She laughed at him. "Because you were a foolish boy – and so clean." Esther spoke softly beside his ear. "You were no threat. Daddy did well from the war; guns made him even richer and bought us sanctuary. I didn't need a trophy husband, so he let me choose you."

"I also promised to bring you to England."

"Took your time." She nibbled the lobe of his ear. "I thought we'd never leave." Esther had hated the heat and the constant clicking of invisible insects. Most of all she hated the soldiers. She said they stank of corruption and beer.

"I had to earn my own way." The touch of her lips lulled him. "Brought you with me."

When he woke again, the flat was dark; he could see his breath as he blew into his hands. The steady background thump of music came from the room above, in the hallway foreign voices shouted. His foot nudged the toy gorilla, now lying on the carpet. One eye mocked him.

Mo had said the rec bonfire would be lit later that evening. It was dusk already. If he went now, then he still had time.

"What the fuck you playing at?" A voice boomed at him from the ground. Gideon looked down from the top of the bonfire, his foot slid along a plank but he managed to keep himself from falling backwards. The bald-headed giant, that Mo had called Keith, shouted again. "Whatever you've got up there, bring it down now!"

Slowly, Gideon climbed down the side of the bonfire. One hand clutched the toy gorilla, its stiff fur piercing his glove like tiny needles. He slipped the other hand into his anorak to curl around the penknife. Keith, or whatever he was really called, must have been waiting for his return. Black swirling patterns covered the backs of Keith's hands. Similar waves of ink twisted around his neck like the tendrils of a monstrous plant.

Gideon blinked carefully, taking in the man's stance, estimating his weight. The man's breathing came in loud wheezes. His eyebrows and stubble were white. He couldn't believe his luck; an old man had come to kill him. In his pocket, Gideon opened out the blade. With his collar down, Keith's wide, white neck shone like a beacon.

Run, whispered Esther. *You are younger, faster. He won't catch you.*

A sudden volley of gunfire, like the rounds from a machine gun, crackled from the direction of the seafront. Keith didn't flinch. Then a trace of golden stars shot into the darkening sky.

"I have to patrol the rec – make sure no silly beggars try planting some surprise fireworks." Keith was still shouting. For a second, the older man's gaze fixed on the cuddly toy. "What you got there? A toy gorilla? Bloody hell, mate, you can't burn that." This was his chance to act. Get in before Keith could retaliate. "I know your type," continued Keith. "You all want to come, but what do you find when you get here? We're just as shit poor. Just as fucked up. This ain't the land you dreamt of, is it mate?" The man balled his tongue, blew out pockmarked cheeks and then spat towards the grass. A fleck of spittle landed on Gideon's arm, leaving a dark patch on the green material. "Go on, mate, you get on home."

Esther leant over his shoulder to peer at the phone. When Mo upgraded to a Smartphone, he let Gideon have his old mobile for nothing. Gideon only used it to contact Mo. "What does he say?" asked Esther.

"Wants me to meet him at the allotment this morning."

"Take me, Papa, please!" Blessing sat at his feet, cuddling his legs.

"I can't – you must go to church with your mama."

"You're frowning," whispered Esther, as she stroked his brow. "What are you worried about?"

"His message was short, like an order. This is not like Mo." He sighed. "If he knew the things I've done – he would not want me for his friend."

Esther knelt at his side to kiss his hand. "Tell him then and let him choose."

At the allotments, Mo met him at the iron swing-gate. The grass cracked like glass under their feet. "Sorry to drag you away from Esther and Blessing on a Sunday," said Mo, not looking at him.

Gideon kept his voice cheerful. "They are at church, so I am happy to help you."

There was little left on the plot to help with. All the turnips had been pulled from the ground, then piled and burned along with the bamboo canes. A circle, coloured in with soot and ash, marked the earth where the fire must have burned. The empty bed where the turnips had been planted was flattened and black lines snaked across it.

"Keith texted me, said there was a problem," began Mo.

"I don't like this man."

"He's a bit brusque, but harmless." Mo gave a sigh. "Heck, he's spotted us."

Keith jogged over to join them. On his head wobbled a red and white striped knitted hat, while a matching scarf guarded his thick neck. After sucking in several gulps of air, he tapped his ear. "All good today. Batteries sorted." Keith spoke normally, no longer shouting like the night before.

"Hey, Keith, thanks for the heads up," said Mo.

"Look, mate." Keith twisted round, eyeing Gideon as he spoke. "You can't burn stuff on these plots. No bonfires allowed. I won't tell, but some of the other beggars would shop you."

"We didn't do this." Mo stared at the blackened soil. "Why would we do this?"

Keith scratched under his nose. He looked down, talking to Gideon's trainers. "Sorry about last night, mate. You scared me, scrabbling about up there as if you wanted to be the guy on the bonfire, thought you were going topple off."

"I have to go," said Gideon. He should give a reason, this was the polite thing to do, but he had to get away from them. They let him leave without calling out any goodbyes. At the gate, he stopped to look back. Keith had moved closer to Mo, too close, a hand rested on the shorter man's shoulder. Mo arched backwards, as if clenching inside.

The hot plate was turned on full. Gideon held the photograph above the glowing red spiral.

"What are you doing?" Esther wore the same blue dress from the photograph, the strappy one that stretched to her ankles showing off her figure. Her stance was proud, with Blessing perched on her hip. The child sucked her thumb, bare legs and feet dangling around her mother's slim body. Both of them stank like the embers of a fire that had been burning all night.

"I wanted you and Blessing to be happy here," he said aloud. "But I have no friends here. I am alone."

You are not alone, Esther whispered.

Yes, he thought, *I am*.

He kissed the photograph, held it closer to the hot plate. A knocking on the door made him hesitate.

In the gloomy hallway, Mo stood holding a yellow felt banana, the same banana that had been attached with Velcro to the toy gorilla. Mo followed him inside as he moved too quickly to sweep back the single curtain covering the flat's only window. He watched as Mo looked around, taking in the tiny kitchen area with sink, fridge and hot plate, and then the mattress and duvet pushed into the corner.

The edge of the photograph lay almost touching the hot plate. Mo snatched it away as one corner began to curl. "You'd better turn that off," he told Gideon, "don't want to start a fire."

Mo took one of the plastic chairs; patting a second he said, "Sit with me, Gideon."

They sat in silence for some minutes as Mo studied the photograph. "Keith found the banana on the path beside the allotment; he reckoned it fell off before you burned the gorilla along with the turnips," said Mo. He let the words settle between them, then touched the base of his throat. "Tell me about the crucifix you wear..."

Gideon slumped in the chair, his head bowed. One hand reached to grip the silver chain around his neck. "I had to make a trip over the border, had to leave Esther and Blessing behind in Kampala. I needed to collect our new papers for England." Raising the cross to his lips, Gideon whispered, "Esther gave this to me for the journey."

"They never left Uganda, did they? You came to the UK alone."

Gideon retrieved the toy banana from under Mo's chair where it had fallen. He did not remember making the bonfire on the allotment, but in his heart he believed Mo spoke the truth. He had wanted to burn the toy, burn all the lies that shouted his guilt. Burn all the memories.

"I am a bad man, have told you many lies, but please do not go to the police. I will pay for the damage to the allotment. If you tell the police, they will find out I am illegal and send me back."

"You never worked as a park-ranger, did you?"

Gideon hung his head. "I was a soldier."

"You told me a lot about gorillas."

"The library has many books. And I borrowed all the BBC DVDs. Sir David Attenborough is my favourite, a very clever man." His breathing deepened as he tipped forwards, rocking onto the two front legs of the chair. "Will you go to the police?"

"No," Mo spoke quietly, as if talking to himself. "I know what it's like to live a fear-filled life. What are you frightened of, Gideon?"

"If I go back, he will kill me. He tried before."

Mo sighed. "Who are you talking about?"

"The father of the boy I killed," began Gideon.

"The green and brown trucks came when I was fourteen. My mother had sent my sisters to meet me as I walked home along the dirt track from school. Out of breath from running all the way, they took my hands and pulled me into the bushes.

We must hide, they told me. Their voices gabbled like a forest stream. *We cannot go home until Mama comes for us.* But I heard the rat-a-tat of gunfire. The sounds cracked the air like fireworks and I knew my mother was in danger. I pushed my sisters down.

Told them to wait for me and then I ran towards my village.

There were two trucks waiting. Soldiers were loading on the boys. They held back the older men with rifles. One man, I don't remember his name, was on the ground, face down. He wasn't moving. The women were wailing and crying. I didn't see Mama.

At fifteen, I first killed a man. There was an attack on our camp. I knew how to use a rifle – took one from a body – and fired into a group of men fighting with machetes and clubs. Closed my eyes and kept firing.

The camp grew like a village. We slept in metal huts and even built proper toilets. Our general wanted to track our business; he wanted us to be modern and efficient. Supporters donated mobile phones and computers. He also brought in a young woman, the daughter of a wealthy sympathiser, to work and manage these computers. This was Esther.

As the war continued, men began deserting. Others died in random attacks. Then another faction made a final move to take control of our sector. The general went out with a scouting party. I stayed behind with Esther. She was very big with my child.

Kengo, one of the older soldiers who had always been kind to me, arrived with a truck and two women: the general's wife and her sister. Our general wanted them taken safely out of the country. "You take Esther with you," I ordered Kengo.

"I'm not leaving without you," shouted Esther. With one hand on her large belly, the other fingered the silver cross around her neck.

I told Kengo to take the mountain track through the national park, then I climbed into the truck to sit with Esther and the women, who squashed against each other for comfort. They did not speak to us.

Several miles along the red dirt track, Kengo stopped to show me the bodies at the side of the road. We recognised our men.

Kengo and I had to check the road ahead. "You must stay in the truck," I ordered Esther.

Esther understood. She took both of my hands and kissed them. For once she had nothing to say.

The road ahead was empty. There was a trail leading into the forest. We followed it to a clearing. Even the birds were silent that morning.

I counted two bodies in the clearing, the general's bodyguards. In the bushes we found three more. Some had been shot, others hacked with machetes. The general was on his back, as if sleeping in the sun. When I pulled him up, half his head fell away. The flies were already feasting, the blood still sticky.

I ran back through the jungle, my rifle slippery in my shaking hands. Kengo followed, jogging and coughing. At the road, the silence was broken by a woman's scream. It came from the trees.

Creeping round the truck, I found the body of the general's wife. Esther was crouched, like a child, still in the back of the truck. The other woman was missing.

The crack of a gun sent birds flying to the sky. A boy in combats walked out of the jungle. He smacked the bushes with his pistol, while his other hand tugged at his open flies. He was taller than me, but only fifteen or sixteen.

Kengo caught up. Between his breaths, he called out, "Chidike, I know this boy."

The boy grinned at me. "Your woman is safe. Put down your rifle. I am a friend."

I could not risk another shot. The first still echoed and the rest of the boy's group could quickly return. Right now he was alone. I laid my rifle in the dirt, keeping my eyes locked on the grinning boy.

Kengo moved behind me. The boy's pistol arm swung up, pointing at Kengo. As I put down the rifle, my other hand had slipped out my knife. It would not slice through bone in one strike, and neither could I risk him firing on Kengo. I sprang on him and slashed the knife into his throat. The boy fell backwards. His hands couldn't stop the blood. Nor could he cry out for help.

"You should not have done that," said Kengo.

Pushing him away, I shouted, "I should have let him shoot you, old man?"

"I know this boy. I know his father." Kengo stood over the twitching body, shook his head. "You should not have killed him."

Blessing was born in the truck as Kengo drove us across the border into Uganda. Esther's father arranged for us to travel to Kampala, where her family were living. We settled with Esther's parents until I earned enough for us to come to England. I ran errands for local businessmen. They were not honest, but paid well.

After four years, I had enough to buy new passports. I had to cross the border to pick up the papers. This kept me away for two days. That is all.

The boy's father tracked me to Kampala.

The fire burned for a whole night. The bodies were laid on the veranda. I counted four. The house servants had fled.

One of the bodies was much smaller than the others.

Without me, the boy's father had taken his revenge anyway. He would hunt me down if I stayed in Africa. I knew Kengo had betrayed me. I do not blame him. I do not expect his information saved his life."

When Gideon fell silent, Mo carefully set the photograph of Esther and Blessing down on the plastic chair where he'd been sitting. Taking off his glove, Mo held out his right hand. Gideon felt the other man tremble as his fingers curled around Mo's.

"Chidike is your real name?"

"It means 'God is strong'. Esther liked that. I chose a new name for my new life in England." He gently squeezed Mo's hand. "Shortly after I first met you in the library, you said you would *put in a good word*."

Mo's mouth twitched. "I meant I could recommend you for a job."

"What is a good word?" said Gideon quickly, before the other man could continue.

This time, Mo gave a soft laugh; he seemed to consider the question carefully before answering. "Friend is a good word."

"Yes." Gideon released Mo's hand. "In Swahili, this is *rafiki*."

"There's nothing to do on the allotment now till spring," said Mo.

Gideon's head drooped, his shoulders sagging as he waited for Mo to explain how they could no longer be friends.

"But next Friday I'll be in the library, usual time. See you there?"

"Yes," said Gideon, his eyes scrunching up. "I will be there."

Mon ami. Friend. *Rafiki.*

In any language, friend was indeed a good word.

OCTAVIA'S GRAVE

The trowel clinked against something solid. Julia stood back, allowing the young woman to clean away enough impacted soil to uncover a hint of bone.

With perfect timing, Professor Marcus Penhaligen arrived at their plot on his morning circuit of the work in progress. His scorched brown arm draped easily across the young woman's shoulders, a hand teasing the white skin of her neck. Octavia swatted it away. A post-doc student from Romania, Octavia seemed to have walked straight out of a fairy-tale, with her pallid complexion and tumbling ebony curls.

"Well, well, Octavia, what have we found?" Marcus crouched beside her and with his own brush began to expose the protruding bone. "Your first grave."

"Julia, I need you to work closely with Octavia on this." Then he spoke softly into the younger woman's ear, "Julia's one of our best gravediggers. This could be one of our most significant finds to date." His hand slipped down to linger along the outline of her breast.

"You seem to be doing a great job without me," Julia boomed after Marcus had moved on again. Tousled, cropped red hair framed her wind-flushed cheeks, clashing with the sagging purple jumper. "What are your thoughts?" she asked, creaking into a cross-legged position.

Octavia took on Marcus's lecturing tone as she recounted her observations. "The orientation suggests this is a Roman burial." She pointed to the dome of the skull, now visible within the earth. "But the actual body is likely to be that of a camp follower, a native Briton."

Julia gave a slight nod, without comment.

"I think it could be a young woman," Octavia added and then hesitated. A weak smile strained her lips, yet the dark eyes flinched as if shadowing a sudden spasm of pain.

The afternoon sun had slunk behind clouds and the temperature was dropping. The girl happily worked away in a plain cotton T-shirt and denim shorts; her Eastern European blood immune to the fickleness of the English seasons.

"Yes, I agree," said Julia. "Any evidence of grave goods?" Octavia shook her head. "And have you had lunch?" Another head shake. "Right, didn't think so." She allowed her voice to sharpen as she slipped into headmistress mode. "Let's get you a hot drink, something to eat and then we can get another couple of hours in before we lose the light."

At dusk, the two women worked together to ensure the grave was covered and protected from the elements. The dampness in the air promised later rain as the flat, grey clouds draped over the dig site. With a fleeting touch to the skeleton's knuckles, Octavia seemed to bid the prostrate girl a silent goodnight.

September sunshine burned off the morning mist to warm the dewy grass and the bare limbs of those diggers who'd removed their top layers. Julia joined Octavia at the graveside close to eleven, purposefully leaving the young woman time to progress the excavation.

Octavia had exposed a significant amount of the skeleton. The skull was breaking free of the clinging earth and the remaining bones were visible. Julia knew they didn't have long before Marcus would appear to appraise their progress.

There was something unusual about the grave.

There were too many bones.

Julia swore out loud.

Octavia sat back. "This is a double burial, I think."

Marcus will be ecstatic, thought Julia. Any unusual finds led to press publicity for the dig and potentially more funding.

On cue, Professor Penhaligen appeared at the head of the grave. He sank down to the same height as the two women.

"Good work, girls." Then he exhaled loudly, "What do we have here?"

"Poor mite died in childbirth," Julia said quietly.

He studied the arrangement of bones. "And the baby died with her."

Octavia added, "The mother is very young, I think."

"Of course," snorted Marcus. "Clearly this is the skeleton of a teenage girl – could be fifteen years or even younger. I'm going to call Jerry in Oxford – need him to come look at this." Marcus stood up but before bounding away he leant down to deposit a forceful kiss on Octavia's forehead. Julia observed the girl flinch at his touch. "Quite marvellous!"

A Labrador would have wagged its tail with doggy joy, but Octavia merely dipped forward to continue her work. Her face was closed, mouth a straight taut line and eyes focused only on the contents of the grave.

Octavia continued to work around the ribcage for several minutes in silence before speaking again. "Who is Jerry?"

"An old Oxford buddy of Marcus', Jeremy Mason, he's now Head of Roman Studies. Also Jerry's an osteoarchaeologist – all of this is right up his street."

"He will be here soon?"

"I think she'll tickle his fancy right enough," said Julia. "Jerry could be onsite by tomorrow."

"We only have the rest of the day with her?" Octavia's voice trembled.

"Afraid so." She put a hand to the girl's shoulder. "This is a significant find and we'll have to relinquish her to the experts." Or vultures, she thought, the men would devour the body, all over again.

The two women worked silently at opposite sides of the grave for the next hour, both engrossed in their target area and internal monologues. Every half hour, Julia would stand, walk around and stretch her back. She watched Octavia working on her knees, continuous without a break to stand or even lift her head.

As Julia paced back and forth beside the grave, Octavia began to talk again. "Does Marcus have any children?"

"Two boys and a girl. All grown and dotted around the country in various colleges." Jack, his eldest, was working on his postgraduate degree and probably the same age as Octavia. Julia did not offer this snippet of information.

Little Jack, bless him, had been the only son and heir in the Penhaligen clan when they were first together. Just starting to toddle when Marcus had announced he would really do it. He would give up his family for her and the coming baby. But the fates had mocked them.

Octavia did not pose the same question to her companion. Dr Julia Owen's spinster, childless, status was openly known and her trademark. Julia contentedly played the part expected of her age and fecundity – at times, the freedom to disappear behind the scatty academic camouflage was a blessed relief. She no longer competed on the sexual battlefield and rejoiced in the liberty that her intellect had brought.

"Marcus tells me you're close to finishing your thesis," said Julia as she sank down to her knees again.

"I am hoping to submit before the end of the year."

"When you have your doctorate, will you return home?"

Octavia hovered over this question. "I don't know what I will do... afterwards."

Julia fetched sandwiches for lunch, which they both ate at one of the wooden benches squatting near the makeshift car park. She also shared her flask of peppermint tea with Octavia, who had declined coffee. A skein of geese beat a path above their heads, calling to one another as they flew westwards.

Octavia ate her sandwich carefully. With one arm across her stomach, she rocked herself gently.

"Are you getting cold?" asked Julia.

"A little, but I'll warm up again when we get back to work."

As Julia climbed down into the pit again, she stopped suddenly, bending forwards. "Octavia," her cry was excited, "look here..."

Their first material find, not bone, but a bead. Julia worked around the find and soon uncovered seven other beads scattered close to the skeleton's wrist bones. "It must have been an amber bracelet." Her face flushed pink, eyes gleaming.

"Like this." Octavia held out her own thin wrist adorned with a bracelet of orange amber hearts bound together by silver links.

"How lovely," said Julia, fingering the warm stones of Octavia's bracelet. "Synchronicity in action."

A fleeting flash of red burned Octavia's cheeks. The women stood in the grave and considered the modern piece of jewellery around Octavia's arm.

Julia asked the girl to take her place and continue excavating the beads, whilst she moved down to the feet of the adult skeleton. Octavia was reinvigorated, her eyes shone and she chattered happily as she worked at the clumps of congealed earth. Her diligence was soon rewarded. A larger object was coming free, resurrecting from the earth, its shape disguised by the cocoon of grave dirt that encased it.

Octavia worked it out of the ground and held it up. The object was metallic, round with a small spoke of a handle.

Julia gasped, "A hand mirror." She scraped away the excess of ancient mud. "This is speculum: an alloy of tin and copper, see how it's been polished to make it reflective." She chewed on her lip. "This is even better than the one found in Whitchurch; it was part of a cremation burial in the Roman cemetery."

"These are high status items," said Octavia. "Maybe she was more important than we thought?"

"I doubt it. I think she's still some low status Briton buried with her few possessions – precious only to her. They are more likely second-hand trinkets given to a favourite whore. Possibly she knew a high-ranking soldier, pleased one of the garrison centurions."

Octavia folded inwards and crumpled onto the grass, eyes closed, a grimace contorting her pretty face.

"How long has this been going on?" sighed Julia.

"Two days. It started as a dull ache, like toothache, now it's like I have a creature ripping out my insides. And… I've been bleeding."

"How much blood?"

"Just spots," the girl mumbled.

Octavia would have to be taken to hospital. Once they abandoned the grave, Marcus would take over.

Julia stood and rubbed the dirt from her hands. "Our work here is done for today. We need to get you some help."

Damp strands of black hair stuck to the girl's forehead, like drawn on curls, as Julia drove Octavia straight to the local hospital.

"How many weeks gone are you?"

Octavia shrugged her shoulders. "I'm not sure."

"Have you done a test? Seen a doctor?"

The girl sat hunched in the passenger seat; eyes closed and head clamped against the headrest. She said nothing.

"Does Marcus know?"

Octavia cried out, "No! He must not know."

Julia gripped the steering wheel, trying not to look at her passenger. "Okay, and I won't tell him. But I will need to call him soon — let him know we've left the dig."

Julia dragged a wheelchair from A and E to the car. Nobody offered help or accompany her. She took charge and deposited the girl with the nursing staff of the gynaecological unit at the hospital. "She may be having a miscarriage." Simple words expressed to the back of Octavia's head.

Her duty was done. She should go home. Eat, run a bath and forget about Octavia and the other pitiful child lying exposed in that grave.

Retrieving enough change from her car to feed the vending machine for caffeine, Julia settled down in the visitor's room and waited. An hour later, a nurse wearing flat, clunky shoes, sought her out. "You came in with Octavia?"

Standing, Julia towered above the nurse. "How is she?"

"Octavia is not having a miscarriage. The embryo appears to have implanted in the fallopian tube; this is called an ectopic pregnancy."

Julia exhaled deeply.

"There doesn't appear to be any internal bleeding but we can't leave her too long." The nurse glanced at her wristwatch. "They'll take her down for surgery in the next hour so you can sit with her until then."

"And the baby?" Julia's voice was flat.

The nurse shook her head. "With an ectopic pregnancy, the embryo has to be removed – there is no chance for the pregnancy to continue." Her teeth were polished and perfect. "Octavia is still young and fit. There is every chance she could conceive successfully again with one fallopian tube. You brought her in at the right time – this type of pregnancy can deteriorate quickly, can be very dangerous for the mother."

Octavia was in a single room. The blinds were closed, shutting out the blackness of the night.

"Do you know what's going to happen?" Julia asked her.

"They explained everything to me."

Julia held her hands together and concentrated upon them. "Don't be angry with Marcus."

"Why would I be angry with him?" Octavia's tone was impatient. "We are both responsible, but I have chosen to leave him out of this. It was coming to an end anyway. I was just another diversion, evening entertainment after a day digging up the past."

The girl's outburst hit a nerve of truth. There was nothing more to say. Julia reached into her jacket pocket, remembering what she had stuffed there in her earlier panic.

Octavia stared as Julia held up the Roman mirror. "You took that?" she said with disbelief.

"I must have put it in my pocket when you collapsed. This mirror held her image until they covered her over. Since then it has had nothing to reflect."

"Do you think she died alone?" said Octavia.

"Marcus is pretty certain the main building is a brothel," Julia began calmly. "Our girl was probably a prostitute living there, surrounded by people who knew what they were doing. Maybe the baby was too big, or her build too slight and they couldn't save her. I'd like to think they mourned her."

Another nurse entered the room, followed by an orderly. It was time to take Octavia down to theatre. Julia trudged behind the entourage that pushed Octavia's bed down several floors to the operating theatre. There was no time to say anything further.

Within two hours, Octavia was wheeled back to her room where Julia still waited.

"She should sleep through to morning," said another nurse she'd not seen before. "Her temperature seems stable but I'll keep monitoring her during the night to ensure she isn't developing any infection."

The nurse brought her a spare pillow. Julia failed to find a comfortable position on the cold, fake leather chair. She closed her eyes, but didn't sleep.

If this girl had been her child, what wisdom would she impart? *End it with Marcus. Finish the doctorate. Focus only on work; immerse body and soul into your career...*

Her own baby had been born on the first day of May. She had already decided to name her Maia, after the Roman goddess. Eventually, the midwife had relented in the face of her pleading. It was against protocol but, for a few minutes, she had been allowed to hold her baby. Thankfully, the starched uniform retreated, leaving Julia and Maia alone together. Such tiny perfect fingers, exquisite little toes and a soft, gingery fuzz on her delicate head.

They told her she was young and fit with plenty of time to try again. But swimming against the tide of age grew too hard. No other chances came again and she accepted her life would be a childless one.

*

The cycle of hospital daily life kick-started early with the clatter of trolleys and the clip-clop of sensible shoes on polished lino. A nurse checked Octavia's vital signs at six-thirty and said to Julia, "She's doing well. Doctor will want to keep her in for another twenty-four hours, ensure she's clear of any infection, then she can go home." *Poor mite*, Julia thought to herself, *home is the last place she can go*. "She shouldn't be on her own. Is there someone to look after her?"

"I will look after her." Surprisingly, it was her own voice, strong and confident, making this declaration.

Mid-morning in the visitors' annex, the vending machine spat out hot, black liquid into a beige cup. A wall-mounted screen flickered silently. It was the local news report: a damp, misty field where two men stood beside a hole in the ground. Marcus, still astonishingly handsome, with his large hands tucked into brown corduroy trousers, enthused to a figure off camera. A shorter man, Jerry Mason, who had put on weight since she had last seen him, swung his arms as if impatient for his turn to speak.

Julia turned away from the screen, barely containing a weary sigh. Octavia's grave was open for business.

IN THE COPPER CANYON

The yellow laces of my running shoe slap against the tarmac. I stop and re-tie them. It's always the left trainer and always at this spot on my route through Bosque de Chapultepec, the largest park in Mexico City. They come undone at the feet of *La Fuente de Tláloc*. The fountain's statue depicts a rain god. His sad, stone-grey eyes stare at the cloudless sky. He is oblivious to the spring blossom sticking to his static body like pale pink snow. I tie a double knot as Elida runs past, her pendulum plait swinging in time with her smooth, easy gait. This is my daily penance, trapped at the fountain by unruly laces, to watch my sister race ahead.

Running is as natural as breathing to my tribe. I close my eyes and suck in a long breath. Altitude isn't the problem. My lungs grew with me in the high copper-coloured canyons of the Barrancas del Cobre.

"You okay?" I can feel Santos's hand on my clammy T-shirt.

"I'll be fine in a minute." I can no longer see Elida. I will have to sprint to catch her.

"We shouldn't run when the air is so poor." Santos scolds me as if I were still a child. "And we really shouldn't be running today."

He means before this evening, before our wedding. Tomorrow I will be back here, in the park, for my morning run and to race my sister. How can he not understand?

With oxygen back in my lungs, I straighten, ready to set off again. Santos takes my hand, kisses the pale heart of my palm. "Gabriela," his voice is heavy. "Let her go."

I surge forwards, my hand tugged free from his lips. "She can't win, especially not today," I say.

Santos calls out but does not follow, "She always wins!"

Mamá had always boasted that Elida was wisely named. With *alas en los pies* — wings on her feet — she lived up to her blessing, as Elida meant the winged one. The fastest girl in our village, in the Rarámuri district even, she was set to marry the fastest boy: Santos. For two years, she had easily beaten the rest of the girls in the harvest fiesta race. Her future and marriage were destined. Elida didn't need a third win to prove she really did have wings on her feet; she could relax into a jog and let another family take the glory for our village. That year it should have been Rosa's turn.

Our grandmother worked the treadle, with toothless concentration, on the black and gold sewing machine to tidy the hem of my dress so it swung above my knees. At ten years old, it was my first fiesta race and Elida and I were to have matching dresses. Mamá had chosen the cloth at a gathering before Holy Week. Flushed pink roses with emerald stems on a blue background, glinting like the jewelled plumage of the forest birds as we ran. Two sisters running for our family.

Elida stood a little too close to Santos while he tied a strip of pink material to the end of her plait, making an elaborate bow. His long black fringe flopped forward, shading his eyes, and he kept pausing to flick it away. At fifteen, he was two years older than Elida; she was taller but always slouched against him to hide this. I tried to block out her silly giggles, concentrating on binding the leather straps of the huaraches around my ankles. My dust-coated toes curled into the flat rubber soles, cut from old tyres Papa had won in a bet at some long ago fiesta. The huaraches moulded to become the soles of my feet, better than any high-tech running shoe, carrying me every day along the canyon-edged paths. They were as good as wings.

Rosa, an older girl from our village, crouched beside me. "You need these tight for a race," she said and began to retie the thin leather straps of my running shoes. Like her two younger sisters, Rosa wore a red and gold striped dress, a matching ribbon woven through her plait. "Run well, Gabriela."

"I will try to make my family proud," I said. Then whispering so that Elida could not overhear, "and I hope you win this year."

"I will do my best." Rosa slowly blinked spidery lashes, staring past me towards my laughing sister. "She can't be allowed to win everything."

On my second lap, Santos is waiting at the fountain. He hasn't moved since I sped off in pursuit of Elida. A taller woman, in patterned Lycra shorts and a cropped top, stands behind him, hands on hips. Her eyes are hidden behind sunglasses, so round and large they mask half her face.

Santos steps out to block my way.

"She's getting away," I shout at him.

"This has to stop," he says, gripping my wrist. "No more, Gabriela. This ends today." Santos nods towards the stranger. "This is the lady you race each day. She is not your sister." He goes on to tell me her name but I don't hear what he's saying. His words soar like eagles above the canyons, spiralling into the haze.

I know this is not my sister.

Elida is gone.

She disappeared when I was ten years old.

The fiesta had continued long into the night. The women fried pans of boiled beans, keeping an eye on the bubbling pots of goat meat, while the men shared stories, drinking their corn beer and swapping bets on the next day, when the boys would race. I dozed, my head in Grandmother's lap as she stroked my hair.

Elida had passed me on her second lap of the race, her pace strong and steady while I snatched for every breath. Rosa trailed behind her like a faithful dog, but every time she drew close then Elida simply lengthened her stride and surged ahead. She won easily.

After the race, Rosa sat with arms around her knees, her head bowed. She refused to eat anything and did not join the other girls when they started to dance around the fires. From Grandmother's lap, I watched Santos sipping his beer, smiling weakly as the men around him told old jokes that we'd all heard before. Finally, exhaustion closed my eyes, pulling me down to sleep. I dreamt of the future, when I would win the fiesta race and be crowned as the fastest girl in the district. In this dream, Santos took my hand and kissed it, making me blush as pink as the roses on my dress.

Once the races were done, training for the next fiesta began straight away. We ran every day, resting only on a Sunday. One morning, I tried to keep up with Elida and Rosa but they soon left me behind on the mountain path, kicking up brown dust as I slowed to a walk. Almost two hours had passed when I jogged back into our village, the dogs were howling and the women calling for the men. Rosa stood crying, surrounded by her family. Elida had not returned. A search party was to be sent out, to retrace our route along the canyon edge. My sister was missing.

I followed Santos to Mexico City as soon as I was old enough to leave our village. Each morning we run together in Chapultepec Park. And now we are to be married, hundreds of miles from the high sierras of the Copper Canyon. We have not shared this with our families and only a few friends from the restaurant where we work will be present. There will be no fiesta feast, as neither of us feel free of the past to celebrate in the old ways of our village.

The woman at Santos's side watches me from behind her sunglasses. Her plait has slipped over her shoulder and I realise there is nothing tied to the end. Her skin tone is much paler than mine, her features rounder. This woman is not from my village.

"I came here to forget Elida," says Santos. He is speaking quietly, his face is close to mine so only I can hear him. "Nobody knows what happened to your sister, but we all believe she is dead. You must let her spirit rest, Gabriela. You will never find peace until you do."

Reflected in the stranger's sunglasses, I glimpse a flash of pink and blue, roses against a dazzling sky, the same dress that my sister and I wore for the harvest fiesta race all those years before.

The yellow laces of my trainers have come undone again; both shoes are loose. I take them off, my socks too, and hand them to Santos. "I'm sorry," I tell him and mean it. I can't marry him. Not tonight. Not ever. I should have stayed in the mountains.

My sister's body was never found, yet I buried her deep. Deep within myself, where she could keep running; free from my jealousy and guilt. Santos believes I come to the park to race a ghost. Elida was older, stronger and faster than me. Stubborn. She demands resurrection. I come to the park to chase down the past. To remember my sister.

The memory of that day rises like air warmed by the sun, burning away the morning mist.

Poor Rosa had suffered the suspicions of our village; she finally left for the city a year ahead of Santos. The old women gossiped that Rosa must have known what had happened. She had been running that morning high on the canyon path. How could she have not seen Elida? Had she seen my sister slip and tumble to her death, did she somehow cause her to fall? At ten years old, they thought me too young, their questions were brief and they paid little heed to my answers, which were stilted and muddled.

The men and boys searched the cliff sides and pathways for days, but there were so many places where Elida could have fallen. When I passed Rosa that morning, she had already given up trying to catch her. Sitting beside the path, resting her head on her knees, she merely pointed out the route my sister had taken. Finding a second wind, I stepped into Elida's dusty footprints as I raced to follow her.

My lungs were exploding when I caught sight of my sister on the path ahead. Elida ignored my shouts, just as she had ignored my cries of pain when she lapped me during the fiesta race. When she ran, Elida lived only for herself. The stone hit the side of her head, much harder than I intended; I only wanted to make her stop and wait for me. She stumbled, her feet twisting awkwardly and then Elida fell forward, flying into empty space. Her arms whirled and clutched at the air. Then she was gone. It took me several minutes to work up the courage to crawl to the edge of the path. I could see nothing but the green and copper-streaked sides of the deep canyon.

Again, I tell Santos that I'm sorry. His mouth tightens into a thin line as the realisation of what I'm saying sinks in. *I do love him,* I say softly, *but he deserves someone better.* Barefoot, I curl my toes to soak up the heat of the paving slabs, already baked by the morning's sun. He holds my trainers to his chest and now I see Elida reflected in his eyes. She stands at the head of the fountain's statue, her hand is raised as if beckoning.

This time she waits for me. Together we run, side by side; our strides match, winged feet beating out a strong and steady rhythm. Above me I hear the screeching cry of an eagle.

ANCIENT WING

The distinctive squeals made Irena look up, the mid-August sun forcing her to squint – even with a hand shading her eyes. High above the village, two buzzards wheeled in a tight circle, gliding with outstretched wings on the summer thermals. Irena smiled, understanding the raptors' unchallenged acceptance that the vortices and air currents would keep them up. She ached to join them.

In several hours, Irena would be leaving, returning home after a lifetime in exile. She chastised herself for wasting precious minutes, daydreaming in the garden, when she still had a list of tasks to tick off. David had taught her the simple pleasure of list ticking and now she carried his obsession like a keepsake.

Cancel the newspapers.

Clothes to cancer charity shop.

Feed Saskia.

Saskia appeared from under the Hebe bush like a tabby ghost, conjured simply by thinking her name. The cat weaved between Irena's bare legs, her white-tipped tail twitching in anticipation of some treat. "Yes, yes," said Irena, "I won't forget to feed you before I go." After all these years, she couldn't stand to touch or be touched by the animal. It was still David's cat.

When Cassandra first left for university, and Irena found herself alone in the house, David had surprised her with the tabby kitten "for company". The arrival of Saskia was a splinter in Irena's heart. David was oblivious to her distaste, couldn't see how she hated and mistrusted the cat. It was then that Irena began to doubt that her husband had ever truly understood what he'd married. Irena began to doubt that she could stay with him

107

after all.

Bury spare key in porch geranium pot.

Turn off hot water timer.

Make sure Cassandra KNOWS key is in geranium pot!

She stayed until Cassandra graduated. Then just a little bit longer to see her daughter settled in a job. Waiting until Cassandra moved in with Alec, her boyfriend, and long enough to ensure the relationship was a pair bond.

David must have seen something in the hunch of her shoulders, heard the longing in her wistful sighs and suspected how she yearned to return to the forests that spread across the mountain side like a vast green stain. He caught her staring at the bird feeders, her fingers forgotten in the stinging hot water of the washing-up bowl, as she dreamed of wading into the cool, black lake where she'd once bathed with her sisters. Irena's husband finally accepted what he had brought back to England and promised they would take a trip, back to the Balkans and to the valley where he'd first enslaved her.

The promised trip had to be postponed when David became sick. The travel plans went permanently on hold, like Irena's dreams, when David moved into the hospice.

Buy roses.

Water hanging baskets.

Stop by churchyard to say goodbye.

Irena shooed Saskia into the kitchen, nudging the cat forward with her toes, and tossed a handful of fish-shaped biscuits onto the lino. "See, I feed you as promised," she said, "you ungrateful monster." The click of the front door latch made Irena straighten quickly. Cassandra was early. Time was running out.

"Oh, Mum," said Cassandra, snatching away the box of cat biscuits, "you're supposed to put them in her bowl."

"Why?" Irena's hands flew up. "It eats baby birds off floor without complaint! The monster kills plenty of things without knife and fork."

Cassandra gathered Saskia into her arms; the cat arched backwards to expose a white bib of fur under her chin. After kissing the offered white throat, she glared at Irena. "She's a cat, Mum, and cats need to hunt. It's an intrinsic part of her genetic wiring, her natural behaviour. She can no more stop killing birds than you can stop making silly lists."

Irena sniffed, but there was pride in her voice as she latched the back door. "You sound like your father. Big words I never understand. Always using the big words." She forced out a smile, pushing down the sadness that threatened to change her mind. "You are his daughter – a true scientist." Irena watched her only child coo and fawn over the cat. When had her little girl become such a beauty? Sprouting from a spindly, clumsy teenager into this confident young woman. Tall and slender like David, with Irena's pale skin. Her blonde, almost white, hair was cropped comfortably short and bouncy – unlike Irena's long dark mass.

"You don't have to go through with this, Mum." Cassandra let Saskia jump down to finish her biscuits. "I know you want to do it for Dad, but we can make a donation some other way. We can have a coffee morning, bake lots of cakes. That's how we raised money for charity at school or Uni. Alec has promised you fifty quid to Cancer Research, whether you do it or not." Her eyes widened and she suddenly gushed, "In fact, I'll double that to a hundred, if you promise *not* to do it."

Shut bedroom window.

Unplug clock radio.

Tell Cassandra she is loved.

Irena wrapped her arms around her precious daughter and whispered against her cheek, a prayer that hung in the air like the echo of gossamer wings.

"Speak English, Mum," said Cassandra pulling back from the hug. "Let's talk about this properly like adults, not descend into mystical chants that *I* don't understand. We can still watch the lunatic birdmen and women leap off the pier. We can have hot dogs and candyfloss, watch donuts spin in the fryer and burn our tongues as we eat them hot with tons of sugar." She frowned, as if she were a toddler again, about to stamp her feet. "You don't even have a costume or proper wings or anything. When you run to the end of the pier you're just going to plummet into the sea. What if you really hurt yourself?"

"Please do not fret for me, Cassandra, I will be safe and you can watch me soar above the waves."

Cassandra sighed and slumped against the breakfast bar. Irena smiled. Her daughter was stubborn, but wise enough to know when a battle was lost. "Okay, then I'll be right at the front cheering you on." Cassandra reached down to her rucksack and pulled out a long, narrow box. She held it out to Irena, saying, "I'm sorry, but after the funeral and everything I completely forgot about this."

Irena hesitated and then took the box. She opened it and gasped.

"Dad asked me to give this to you, after he... after..."

"I know."

Cassandra's voice became soft, hushed and reverent. "It's in excellent condition, incredibly well preserved, and I'm not sure he should have kept it."

Irena was puzzled by Cassandra's words. Inside the box lay a single white feather, but how would her daughter know its significance?

"The fossil," explained Cassandra, lifting the feather to reveal a stone slab beneath. "It's a fossilised feather from an *Archaeopteryx* specimen. At bedtime, Dad used to read from his palaeontology books – I never got fairy tales – and he taught me all about *Archaeopteryx*."

"Ancient wing," said Irena quietly, trailing the feather along the back of her arm.

"Yes, that's right. He must have told you the same stories! In Greek, *Archaeopteryx* means ancient wing. It was a dinosaur about the size of a raven and thought to be a transition species between dinosaurs and birds. I think the other feather is from some species of swan. I'm not sure why he kept the two together."

"David was on a dig in my country, hunting for his fossils, when we met." Irena suddenly felt the need to sit and sank onto the nearest kitchen stool. "I should have trusted him, should have known that he really loved me."

Leave rings in envelope with letter to Cassandra.

Take out rubbish.

Tell Cassandra the truth.

Before he finally became unconscious and slipped away, David had urged her to tell Cassandra the truth. "Tell Cassandra how we met on the lakeshore. She must know what I took from you. Tell her how I tricked you, how I made you stay."

Cassandra kissed her forehead. "Of course he loved you, Mum. Don't say such silly things."

"I think he meant for you to keep the fossil," said Irena. She held the feather against her cheek. "But this belongs to me."

The DJ's voice boomed brash and cheery from the loudspeaker, announcing Irena's name and charity. She stepped forward to face the edge of the pier. The crowd clapped and whistled; she could hear Cassandra's voice near the front, cheering her on. Curling her toes, Irena felt the warm wooden slats, baked dry by the recent heat wave. The white linen sundress hung loosely and would allow her to run freely.

Tell Cassandra the truth.

Time had run out. Irena had let her daughter chatter on as they'd driven to the seafront. She realised Cassandra was calming both their fears with inane anecdotes about her workmates and what Alec had said at breakfast. It was the last time she would hear her daughter's voice and couldn't bear for her to stop. Soon Cassandra would know the truth anyway.

Glancing at the cloudless sky, Irena could see them flying low over the South Downs, heading silently towards the sea: her sisters were coming for her, coming to take her home. Closing her eyes, she could hear the rhythmic beat of their ancient wings, a song she knew by heart, as the lamentation of swans flew closer to the pier.

Irena had been bathing alone, without her sisters, on that morning when David came to spy on her at the lake. Stealing her wings had bound Irena to the Englishman until the day he returned her freedom. Back in England, they married and Cassandra was born. Irena grew to accept her earthbound life, grew accustomed to her heavy, plodding frame and clumsy limbs, learned to live without her wings.

In returning the feather, David was setting her free. Irena had tried to explain that she could have taken back her wings at any time, but he was sleeping, already moving on without her. He had never truly imprisoned her. She loved him, her mortal husband, and had chosen to stay with him out of love.

Irena held out her arms, flexing her long pale fingers, and began to run. The crowd whooped, chanting her name. Her bones became hollow. Her body was light, almost weightless, her muscles tight and strong, with outstretched wings she felt like an angel glowing white hot in the sunlight. Salt spray tingled on her lips and a gentle westerly breeze rippled the primary flight feathers, lifting her upwards.

Twisting her long neck round to look one last time for Cassandra, Irena saw a rush of people surge to the end of the pier. Shouts and screams echoed after her as the crowd now stared down into the water, searching for the bird woman who'd leapt into the sea. But her daughter stood alone, looking out across the waves. Cassandra was watching the family of swans as they flew over the coast, one hand shading her eyes, while the other was raised into the air, like a salute, or perhaps in farewell.

MONSTERS

The monster came to live under my bed when I was ten years old, before we moved out of Uncle Toby's. Mum wouldn't let me have a pet, in case it triggered one of Megan's allergies. Not even a goldfish, a stick insect, or a tank of giant snails. I wanted a puppy with sharp snapping teeth to snarl at Uncle Toby, or a kitten with uncut claws that could scratch out a warning in the paintwork of his van. A monster, I soon realised, was better than any pet.

Ravi, my best mate, lived next door and didn't believe in monsters. After school one day, I dared him to look under my bed. "I can't see anything," he said, stretching out a skinny arm as far as he could.

"Right at the back, near the wall." I was beside him, staring straight into the monster's golden eyes.

Suddenly, Ravi wriggled backwards like a clumsy snake, yelping as his head bashed against the bed frame. He leapt onto my duvet and swore at me in Hindi. Then, switching back to English, he screeched, "What the hell is that, Mark?"

"Did you see it?"

"It's scrunched into a ball like a hedgehog and shaking all over." Ravi's voice trembled. "It looked terrified." I could see knucklebones straining through his skin as he gripped his hands.

"You look pretty scared yourself," I said, a little unkindly, since I'd begged him to come and prove I wasn't going mental like Megan. "What do you think it is?"

"Nani must come and see it. Nani knows about everything."

Ravi's grandmother lived with his mum, dad and Ravi's three brothers. She didn't speak any English but always waved to me from the porch, surrounded by chilli and tomato plants, when I came home from school.

After Ravi left to fetch his grandmother, I crouched down to peer back under the bed. The monster's amber fur felt soft against my face. A gentle purr rumbled from deep within its belly, as I stroked the scaly spines along the creature's tail. There was no need to say anything out loud. I could calm the monster with my thoughts.

I hoped Ravi would return quickly, before Mum arrived home with Megan. On Tuesdays, Mum took my sister to see her special doctor. Mum said the doctor was helping Megan to find her voice again. Until she started school, Megan was a "right little chatterbox", Mum's words, and then suddenly all her words fell out, just like Granddad's hair before he died. If I sat close to the banisters at the top of the stairs, some evenings I could hear Mum talking to Uncle Toby in the kitchen. I never heard what he said back to her, only the hiss and crack of a ring pull after he took a can from the fridge. The special doctor, I knew this meant psychiatrist, reckoned starting school had been a *traumatic event* for Megan and so she simply stopped talking all together.

At night, when Mum and Uncle Toby had gone to bed, I took my pillow and slept beside the monster. Its thoughts echoed mine. Adults were stupid. None of them considered that Megan had stopped talking weeks before she started Primary School, but only days after we moved in with Uncle Toby.

It took several minutes for Ravi's grandmother to creak down onto her knees and then to shuffle forwards and lower her grey head beneath the bed. At first she was silent. Then she began clicking her tongue as if calling a horse. Ravi sat cross-legged in the middle of the bed, while I waited beside the old woman, eager to hear her pronouncement. Her lemon sari smelled of sunshine.

We both had to help her stand up again. The bed sighed as Ravi's grandmother sank down. Ravi gently eased her feet back into the slippers that had fallen off under the bed.

"Does she know what it is?" A thousand questions fluttered in my head, all clamouring to take flight.

The old lady talked fast, without taking in air. When she finally stopped, Ravi shushed for me to keep quiet, so he could organise her outpouring into a sensible translation. "Nani says you are blessed," he began. "It has chosen to live with you; this is a very lucky thing. For you and all your family."

"But what is it? Is it a monster?" Ravi translated my question. Her bony fingers flicked the side of my head and a rapid gush of Hindi swept over me. "Ouch! Hey, that hurt," I cried.

"Silly boy," said Ravi, smirking, "there is no such thing as monsters."

I flinched as her hand came towards me again, but this time she pressed it flat to my T-shirt over my chest.

"She says the only monsters are in here." Ravi laughed. "Nani means inside your heart."

"Yeah, I get that, clever dick. What does she mean by that? That I'm a monster?"

He shook his head. "Monsters live in the hearts of men. Mostly they are sleeping like pussycats in the sun, but some are fearless tigers, driven mad with the urge to do bad things."

Ravi's eyebrows crinkled as his grandmother continued talking. He screwed a finger into the side of his head. "I think she needs to visit your sister's doctor," he murmured to me. "Nani is a bit confused."

"Why? What's she saying now?"

"Your creature is very rare. She has heard stories but never seen one herself, or heard of anyone who has. She thanks you for letting her see its white feathers and emerald eyes; it is truly

117

beautiful." He shrugged his shoulders. "That's not what I saw under your bed."

"But can I keep it as a pet?"

This time, Ravi flicked me. "Did you not listen, silly boy? Nani said it has chosen you."

Did that make me its pet?

"What's going on, Mark? What are you all doing up here?" Crap. I'd forgotten to listen out for Uncle Toby's van. Typical, just for once he'd turned up before Mum and Megan. "Something stuck under the bed, mate?"

He dropped to the floor, turning his head sideways to squint into the gloom. Ravi spoke quietly to his grandmother. She nodded; then they both stepped over Uncle Toby's legs and scurried from the room.

"What the f—?" His voice leapt into a screech, as he reappeared with a bloody line across his cheek. "Vermin went for me. Looks more like a demon with those bleeding red eyes and spiky black fur." He wiped a hand across his mouth. "I've got a spade in the van, that'll flush the bugger out."

I was considering if I could drag the chest of drawers over to barricade the door shut. If I could keep Uncle Toby out of my bedroom, then the monster was safe.

Mum walked in as I was tipping socks and underpants onto the floor. "Mark, what have you been up to? Toby says you've got some wild animal living up here." Megan followed her in and immediately sank down to her knees. "No, Megan, get away! Uncle Toby said it was vicious."

I grabbed Mum's arm, giving Megan time to disappear up to her ankles under the bed. The room was silent for a heartbeat and then the monster began to sing. There were no words, just strange, sweet sounds that made me think of the seaside, of ice cream and Megan laughing. I'd forgotten how Megan's giggles made Mum smile.

After several minutes, Megan rolled out. She held a long golden feather, giggled and spoke for the first time in weeks. "Mark's monster is pretty. It sang to me."

Holding a garden spade like a warrior's spear, Uncle Toby pushed past Mum into the bedroom. On seeing him, Megan stood in front of the bed. At first she just pointed, but then she started screaming. The screams soon became howls. From under the bed the monster joined in.

We moved out so quickly, I never had time to say goodbye to Ravi or his grandmother. And we never saw Uncle Toby again. Megan regained her voice, to the point of irritation, becoming Mum's chatterbox again.

The monster stayed with me, as Ravi's grandmother promised, moving with us wherever we lived. When I heard my sister sobbing in the night, I'd sneak her into my room. Under the bed, we crawled to curl either side of the monster; squashed against its soft warmth, we slept safely.

THE WEIGHT THEY LEFT BEHIND

The glossy cover of the clinic's brochure mirrored the view now before him. Rex appraised the whitewashed lighthouse fused to the cliff side, the glass turret with its Cyclops lens revolving silently. Edna had sent off for the brochure, announcing: "We can use the money your dad left," as if it really were a joint decision. The brochure contained photographs of satisfied clients, posing alongside cardboard cut-outs of their former selves, the blurb claiming how their lives had changed forever once they'd started on Dr Excelsior's revolutionary diet.

Edna had taken over the driving for the last stage of the journey into North Devon, as Rex had polished off a large glass of Rioja over lunch. At the roadside pub he mused, "It'll be some bloke in a lab coat slapping your knuckles with a leather belt every time you reach for a biscuit. I'm not having electrodes wired to my genitals."

"Would you notice if they did?" Edna had replied, pulling the cheese board towards her.

When they finally arrived at the lighthouse, there was no sign on the solid green door announcing it to be Dr Excelsior's famous clinic. The sat nav had given up two miles back, when Edna turned the Volvo down the single-track road, pockmarked with potholes, sloping scree on one side and a plunging drop into the sea on the other. The granite steps down from the car park were almost vertical. Would they ever make it back up? Not unless the weekend worked its promised miracle, and they both shed a married lifetime of accumulated weight, or somebody from the clinic carried their bags to the car.

"Are you sure this is it?" said Rex.

Edna folded chubby arms over the shelf of her chest. "It's a lighthouse, monkey brain."

Before their tenth wedding anniversary, her pet name for him had been Puppy Boy, because of his big brown eyes. She'd once been his Sweet Kitten, because of how she purred with delight when he kissed her. Once they stopped counting the anniversaries, he started calling her Edna.

Across the Bristol Channel, low-slung rain clouds masked the Welsh coastline. As a boy, Rex loved to draw seascapes where the sea and sky blurred around a lighthouse tower, banded red and black, its beam scorching the paper. The Aga-warmed air of the kitchen infused with cinnamon and nutmeg, crayons rolling into flour drifts while his mother baked scones, Victoria sponges spilling crimson jam, or his father's Sunday favourite: roly-poly suet pudding.

A buzzer on the wall summoned the clinic's receptionist, a willow-thin brunette who swept them inside and quickly showed them to their suite. Oddly, they had separate bedrooms but there was an adjoining door, which the receptionist explained would be left unlocked since they were a couple. Within an hour, Rex and Edna were swathed in pale lemon bathrobes, flopping about the hardwood floors in slippers and awaiting collection by a dedicated member of the Team.

Tony came for Edna. He towered above her, solid broad shoulders and a thick unmoving neck, making Rex think of a James Bond henchman. While Lucy, her blond ponytail swishing in synchrony to the rhythm of her tight round bottom, cupped Rex's elbow. She led him to a square, low-lit room containing a single chair, all stainless steel and black leather, disturbingly similar to the one at the dentist's. Electrical leads dangled from the ceiling, directly above where the top of his head would soon rest. At least they couldn't stretch to his crotch – or so he hoped. Lucy motioned for Rex to sit.

She made eye contact and smiled. "There's nothing to worry about, the process is completely painless."

Rex blinked quickly at the mention of pain. His stare stuck on the wires, now untwisting like Medusa snakes. "What's going to happen?" he said.

"Until the patent application is successful, I can't divulge the exact details of Dr Excelsior's technique."

A panel slid up in the white wall beside him to reveal a flat screen.

"I have the questionnaire results that you completed online," continued Lucy.

To keep Edna happy, he'd gone along with her idea to book the clinic for their anniversary weekend. Any time spent together was usually defined by where and what they ate. He'd secretly been relieved that Edna had recognised that maybe their dining habits needed to change and the lighthouse clinic could be the start of a new life for both of them. The questionnaire had comprised of an extensive list of food and drink, each with a delicious photograph, trailing across multiple screens and with additional space for comments. Rex wished he could remember exactly what he'd clicked.

Moist fingertips lightly held both sides of his face. "Please look at me, Rex. We're going to play a word association game, a bit of fun to find out your eating habits. This afternoon, you will meet Dr Excelsior."

"What about my wife?"

"She'll be meeting Dr Excelsior this morning." Lucy squeezed his arm. "You'll see her at lunch."

The wires entwined into a rigid halo around his head, ends pulsing with light. Rex became aware of images flashing on the screen in the wall but didn't dare move.

"Listen to my voice and let your thoughts go where they wish." Lucy leant close to his left ear and whispered an indistinct word.

Rex began to imagine a pint of beer, dark old ale with a creamy white froth. He could smell hops mingling with wood smoke, heard the spit and crackle of logs and thought of the hearthside table, his favourite spot in *The Red Lion*.

Lucy whispered again. Rex licked his lips, tasting blackberries and the fruity tang of a Merlot. He saw Melissa, his first serious girlfriend. Fox-red hair tumbled over freckled breasts, as she lay naked on the tiny bed in his university bedsit, giggling as he wrestled off skinny jeans. *When had he last worn denim jeans?* Now he lived in sweatpants with elasticated waists.

"Here comes the final word for this morning's session," said Lucy. She leant in close again, her minty breath blowing into his ear.

Rex was back home, at the oak table in his mother's kitchen. She was popping out golden-topped scones onto a wire tray. Dad was stomping damp wellies, criss-crossed with hay, on the porch. Meg, the Border collie, pushed a cold nose into Rex's palm, her tail thumping the table leg.

"And we're done." Lucy's voice resonated like a gunshot. "You must be ready for lunch."

Rex was astonished to discover over two hours had elapsed since he'd sat in the chair. He was ravenous.

Lucy waved Rex towards the luncheon table. A bowl of jacket potatoes steamed at the centre. "Eat as much salad as you like."

She left him to eat alone with Edna, who was already tucking into a potato. There were bowls of coleslaw, mayonnaise infused tuna, heaps of yellow grated Cheddar and slabs of aromatic blue cheese. Surprisingly, Edna had left the cheese untouched; her plain baked potato surrounded by a sea of red and green lettuce leaves. Not even a dollop of butter oozed on top.

"How was your morning?" said Rex.

Edna looked up from her plate, mouth full of greenery. For a second, her eyes were blank.

He emptied a dish of chilli onto his potato; it flowed over the sides like red-hot lava. "Don't you fancy the cheese?" Stilton was her favourite.

"Cheese?" Edna repeated the word, rolling it around in her mouth. Each time it sounded different, as if she were trying it out for the first time.

Rex gave up after that. He should know by now never to attempt conversation when there was food present. It had been a long time since his wife had paid any attention to what came out of his mouth when there were more interesting things to stuff into hers.

For dessert, Rex was amazed when Edna ignored the fudge cake, usually her pudding of choice, instead settling back at the table with a cup of peppermint tea.

"I feel lighter already," she said, her cheeks flushing. "Tony reckons half a stone. Maybe more by the end of the day."

Before Rex could tell her that was impossible, the two assistants reappeared in the doorway.

It was time for him to meet Dr Excelsior.

Back in the dentist's chair, Rex eyed the leads with suspicion. Once again they writhed above his head like snakes about to strike. Dr Excelsior stood behind him, only visible from his reflection in the wall-mounted screen. The little man was a copycat Gandhi, with liquorice black eyebrows and matching moustache. His hands were hidden behind his starched white coat.

A table had been placed underneath the window. It held three objects: a pint of beer, a glass of red wine and a lopsided scone.

"Look," said Rex, "before we go any further, I need to understand what's happening. How exactly does this diet work?" Edna hadn't given anything away at lunch about her treatment session. Now he regretted not bothering to search out his glasses and read the small print at the back of the brochure.

The circling wires stiffened, then latched onto his scalp. Rex didn't feel anything, but was aware of a humming sound as if the leads were singing. He frowned as his head bubbled with terms such as cognitive process, linear association and others he didn't even recognise as words. Dr Excelsior's lips were hardly moving.

Lucy picked up the pint glass; a froth of beer splashed onto her sleeve. "One sip, that's all you need and then Dr Excelsior's procedure will eradicate the substance from your palette. You will no longer crave hops in any form. Beer and any associated foods or snacks will cease to exist in your life."

Rex had read the clinic's blurb but didn't believe a word of it. He was certain Edna's odd aversion to cheese over lunch was temporary. More likely her faking a bout of newly discovered willpower to justify the weekend's expense. Rex had fancied a painting retreat, something they could do together without involving food.

The sweet tang of barley hit his nostrils as she brought the beer glass up to Rex's lips. Images of *The Red Lion* flickered on the screen in the wall like a slideshow on a digital photo frame. Steak and ale pie steaming on the fireside table. Pastry flakes in his lap.

"I'll never want another pint?" said Rex.

Lucy smiled. "One sip is all you need."

He wanted to push the glass away, but his arms wouldn't move. They may as well have been strapped to the chair. The humming leads prickled on his scalp. On the screen, flashing images merged to a multi-coloured blur, reminding Rex of a recent disastrous visit with Edna to the Tate Modern. He wanted to spit out the foul substance contaminating his mouth. Was she trying to poison him?

"Try this," said Lucy, offering him the wine glass.

"Oh, that's better." Rex drank the wine, but then began to retch. "God, no, that tastes like engine oil." As he sprayed Lucy's apron with blackcurrant spittle, he caught sight of the screen now jumping with indistinct shapes. The pictures flashed so quickly he couldn't make sense of the story.

Dr Excelsior stepped forward, holding the plate. The scone had been sliced in half, spread with strawberry jam and clotted cream. Rex wanted to protest, tell them the jam should go on last, when Lucy squeezed his arm. On the screen, the film slowed to normal speed. Was that his mother? He felt Meg's wet nose press his palm. Heard his father ask if the tea was brewed. He blinked several times, causing a teary dribble to run under his nose.

Lucy whispered something to Dr Excelsior and he returned the plate to the table. The wires retracted from Rex's head to disappear back into the ceiling.

"We'll continue tomorrow," said Lucy, "and identify some alternative triggers for you."

Rex was overcome with a sudden urge to hug her. Silly to get so emotional over a scone. "Thank you," he said, almost sobbing.

Edna chose to eat dinner in her room after her sessions with Dr Excelsior, so Rex ate alone at the long, thin dining table. He pondered on where the other guests were, as he had not seen anyone other than Edna and the staff since their arrival at the clinic. Sipping his sparkling water, he watched the lighthouse beam slice the darkening sea.

On the way to breakfast the following morning, Rex met Edna heading for the treatment room. Her shoulder edged away as she waddled past without acknowledging him. "Good morning to you too," he muttered. The silent treatment should have been a blessing, but this was supposed to be a weekend of bonding as they lost weight together.

Tony brought him a plate of scrambled eggs.

"May I ask about my wife's trigger foods?" said Rex. "Do you know what Dr Excelsior selected for her?"

The henchman glanced towards the door. "I shouldn't really say."

"Chocolate, I expect." Rex grinned. "And cheese! She lives for cheese."

Tony relaxed a little. "The usual suspects. Most guests select all the naughty carbs. The odd thing was she specifically asked for a slice of traditional wedding cake, royal icing and all the trimmings, along with a glass of bubbly."

Rex nodded slowly and put down his fork. "Sounds a bit strange, but I want to change my selection for today's session. Can I have exactly the same as my wife: wedding cake and champagne?"

"Sure, if that's what you want," said Tony. "I'll let Lucy know."

Rex bounded up the steep steps to the car park swinging his suitcase. Sucking in the warm salt-breeze he pulled at the waistband of his trousers, which had started to slip. The cloudless sky was a broad brush-stroke of cobalt blue. His mobile phone jangled in his pocket.

"Hello Mum," he sang out, answering the call. "I'm just leaving. Should be with you before lunch." He let her chatter on while his mood soared higher. "You've been baking, brilliant!"

As Lucy had promised, the taxi was waiting for him. The driver was a woman; slim and tanned with short brown hair. She welcomed him with a dimpled smile. He wondered if she wouldn't mind stopping off in Porlock, where he could buy a sketchbook and some basic watercolours. The urge to paint was overwhelming. A vague memory stirred Rex's thoughts. He'd arrived at the clinic with another woman. She'd driven him there. Rex struggled to recall her name; she'd been red-faced, fleshy and rather morose. No, it couldn't be the same woman driving because the other car had been a silver Volvo. He was certain of that. This time it was a red Nissan, gleaming in the morning sun like a glacé cherry.

BOOK OF THE DEAD

It was the morning after a typical Friday night and the pub stank of stale beer and old man's sweat. Liam found Rosie sitting at a table in the bar. She had made herself a mug of black coffee, which stood untouched, alongside a slice of stiff white toast. Her rucksack sat propped on the chair beside her; a silent companion.

"You'll have to cover tonight on your own," she told him. "I'm not staying." On another chair lay his scrapbook. Liam wanted to snatch it away, but Rosie beat him to it, saying, "I stepped on this when I got up; it was beside your bed."

"That's private," he said.

Her lip trembled as she turned the pages, the newspaper cuttings crackling like dried leaves. Faces of women stared out. "They caught this bloke twenty years ago, yet you're still fixated with him. This is so fucked up, Liam. Why exactly do you keep a book full of dead women?"

The scrapbook fell open to a page where a photograph of the Playboy's first victim was glued above columns of shouty newsprint. Her fair hair was scraped back from her face, making her look more like a teenager than the wife and mother she had been. It was the only photograph Liam had ever seen of her.

The killing spree had begun along with the millennium, the first murder recorded in January 2000, then one a month until he was caught and charged in July. Miss July, nicknamed by the tabloids, had managed to scream for help, causing her attacker to run off. DNA sampling and a door-to-door search finally identified and caught him. A local man. Late-forties, living with his terminally ill mother, who had unwittingly provided her son with numerous alibis when previously questioned. The short balding man had looked nothing like a playboy, but Liam didn't want to talk about him.

Rosie tapped Miss January's picture with her finger. "This is well spooky. She worked here, behind the bar. Just like me, pulling pints in this backstreet piss-hole. He got her as she walked home, poor cow. Strangled with the cable from his bedroom TV. But I guess you know the details by heart, since this lives under your bed."

Rosie closed the scrapbook and shoved it across the sticky tabletop. Liam gathered the dead women into his arms, cradling them against his chest. She stood up quickly, her chair toppling backwards, and pulled on her rucksack. "Do you get off on reading this stuff? Fuck's sake, Liam, I just thought you were shy. A twenty-nine-year-old virgin is weird, but this is too creepy for words."

He watched Rosie walk out of the pub. Didn't try to stop her.

Mam had let him drag his duvet down to the living room. He was tucked under Spiderman on the settee watching videos. This was a special treat, because he was sick and because he was going to have to be a big brave boy for the evening.

"A dose of Calpol will help to bring your temperature down," said Mam. She shook the bottle of strawberry pink medicine. He swallowed the spoonful without complaint; it was sickly sweet but in a good way. "Your dad can't turn down another night-shift. I'll pop back before closing to check on you." She kissed his forehead. "How's your throat?"

"S'okay." When he swallowed, it was like his mouth was full of twigs.

Mam lit up a cigarette, then tucked her lighter behind the clock on the mantelpiece. She wasn't allowed to smoke behind the bar at the pub. "Shall I bring you back some crisps?"

He smiled weakly. "Prawn cocktail, please." Crisps, even with a sore throat, were a treat.

Mam cupped his cheeks in her hands. "Look at this angel face. Butter wouldn't melt."

She slipped on her coat, the black mackintosh with the belt missing, pulling off the velvet scrunchie so her hair tumbled loose down her back (she always wore it down for work), and then walked out of the house.

On Friday night, not long after closing, Rosie had climbed into his bed. Her room was freezing, and she couldn't sleep. He'd just woken from a dream about Mam where he remembered the colour of her scrunchie: emerald green. But he couldn't remember the colour of her eyes. The image in his scrapbook was monochrome, making her eyes a dull grey. Just like all the other dead women in there. That was the only image he had of her. Nothing came after that photograph, everything before that his dad had burned in a metal dustbin, feeding a day-long bonfire with her clothes, make-up, and magazines, all the stuff that smelled like Mam.

"You okay?" Rosie rolled over to face him, her blue eyes wide with concern. "Bad dream?"

This was always the worst time, when he woke in the night and remembered all over again. How Mam had left him with his comics and videos, and a father who couldn't cope without her.

Rosie had turned up for the evening shift at the pub with a rucksack almost as tall as her. She'd been kicked out of her bedsit, she explained. The owner accused her of doing hard core shit, when all she ever smoked was a 'recreational joint'. When the bastard had started pawing her, offering an exchange of services, Rosie packed up what she could and left. All this came out at top speed, with tears following. Liam suggested she took the spare room. He lived onsite, rent free, as the landlord figured it was cheaper to let a big, bearded bloke sleep there as a deterrent, rather than fix the expensive alarm system.

Her hand snaked down his body and inside his boxer shorts. "I can do something to help with the nightmares," Rosie said sleepily.

Liam gently lifted her hand up onto his chest where he hoped she couldn't feel his heart thudding. "No. Please, Rosie, I don't want that."

Propping herself up with her elbow, she studied him. "Is there any part of you that isn't covered in tattoos?" Rosie stroked his beard. "What are you hiding from?"

When they worked a shift together, Liam envied Rosie's confidence. How she joined in the bar banter, standing no nonsense from the punters and slapping away the hands that lingered on her backside as she moved between the tables collecting empty glasses. He always imagined Mam had been just like that in the pub.

"I'm thinking of getting one. A tattoo. Does it hurt?" said Rosie.

Liam couldn't answer. He didn't remember. Each image inked into his skin had brought only temporary oblivion. If it had hurt, then he'd probably deserved it.

He thought of Mam, her papery face buried inside the scrapbook under his bed. When he couldn't sleep, she was always there for him. He could talk to her and the other women, share his hopes and dreams. Like how he really fancied Rosie, but didn't dare make a move.

Now Rosie was in his bed, making a move, and all he wanted was to talk with Mam.

"I'm sorry, it's just I've never done that," he said, staring up at the ceiling.

"I like you, Liam, you've never tried it on with me." She kissed his cheek. "We can just cuddle. Would that help you sleep?"

Liam had always slept alone. "Maybe," he said.

Rosie didn't return for Saturday evening and Liam was on his own, just as she'd threatened. Her presence in his bed had confused him, and now her absence was unsettling. She had been kind, patient and understanding about his shyness. Until she'd found his scrapbook.

It was a quiet night, a month after Christmas, when the punters had little to spend. The trendy town centre bars sucked in the students and young professionals, leaving Liam with his flat cap regulars and a booth squashed with four loud blokes on their sixth round. They kept calling him over whenever a refill was needed. The local newspaper was open on their table. A headline announced: RELEASE IMMINENT FOR PLAYBOY KILLER. Everyone in the pub, except Liam, had been talking about this all day. The centre spread featured the familiar headshots of his six victims, Miss January to Miss June.

Liam placed two fresh pints on the table, then collected the empty glasses, one in each hand. He tried to ignore her. She looked out of the newspaper, her dead eyes searching for him. This wasn't the time to talk with her. The men batted opinions back and forth like verbal tennis. The key topic was: should the Playboy, now with only months to live, be let out to die a free man? Their voices merged, becoming all the chants that Liam had heard as a little boy. Nine years old and waiting for his mam to come home.

Life should mean life.

Let him rot inside.

Like the Ripper.

He was on a mission too. Hated prossies.

Liam stood there, at the edge of their conversation, silent and waiting for the untruths to surface. There was a lockup in the yard where Liam had found a rusting can of ancient rat poison on the top shelf. It was probably illegal, no longer humane. Several drops could end up in their next round. On the house.

One of the men leant over, tapping at his mam's face.

She worked here. Behind the bar. Nice piece of skirt...

Liam slammed the pint glass down onto the newspaper, which left an unfortunate arc of beer slicing through Miss April. Splinters of glass spun in all directions. As the men blustered and swore, he raised the jagged edge – pointing it directly at the beetroot-faced man who'd spoken last.

"Liam!" Rosie tugged his arm down, then steered him towards the bar. To the men she said calmly, "We're closed, so fuck off."

When they were alone in the pub, Rosie rolled back the sleeve of her sweatshirt to show him the reason for her late return to the pub. She'd got a tattoo. The initials R and L were entwined, inked within a dodgy Celtic knot on the inside of her wrist. The symbol made Liam's skin tingle. A scary, but good, tingle.

What did Rosie's tattoo mean? Liam would have to ask Mam. Was she a bit flaky? Flaky. That was a word he remembered Mam using. A lot. *Seems a bit flaky.*

At Rosie's feet was Liam's sports bag. Red and white, the colours of his favourite football team before he'd turned ten. "I've packed your stuff," she said. "Even that creepy scrapbook. I know why you keep it." Her rucksack stood by the pub's exit. "I'm taking the bus to the station. Come with me."

"Where?" said Liam. He didn't ask why she'd come back, but he was glad she had.

"Anywhere but here."

Outside the pub, a damp drizzle had made the pavement slippery. Liam locked up, then Rosie took the keys from him and pushed them through the letterbox. They made a satisfying clunk as they hit the terracotta tiles.

"The tattoo," he said to Rosie, "did it hurt?"

"Doesn't everything?"

At the bus stop, a woman clicked past on sharp heels, silvery-blonde hair dripped down the back of her coat like a stream of moonlight. She stopped, and walked back to them. "Have you got a light?" She held out a cigarette towards Liam. The long hair was misleading. Facing him, he could see she was at least fifteen years older than Mam.

Liam hesitated. Flustered, he offered her all he had on him — Mam's old lighter; possibly the last thing she ever held and the one thing he'd saved from going into the bonfire. When she flipped the lid, a tiny flame shot up. It still worked, after all those years. The woman lit her cigarette, mumbling, "Thanks," then set off again.

The road was empty of traffic or pedestrians, the dank air still and silent. Liam glanced nervously at Rosie. "Maybe I should walk her home?"

She touched his hand with ice cold fingers. "You can't save your mother. I know every night, in your dreams, she never makes it home."

The woman was heading for Cable Street. Mam would've carried on to the corner of Market Way, then taken a left turn into their road.

"She only popped out because I was ill," said Liam. "Wanted to check on me before last orders."

"It wasn't your fault."

That's what everyone had told him. Everyone except his dad.

Liam took off his hoodie to pull it around her bony shoulders. The digital display inside the shelter showed their bus was due in four minutes. Rosie's canvas shoes were too thin. They were both woefully underdressed. *You'll catch your death*, Mam's voice echoed inside his head.

"Shit," he said, panic rising. "She kept the lighter. It belonged to my mam, I have to get it back."

"There isn't time. This is the last bus, Liam." He heard desperation in her voice, and something else, something broken. "Don't leave me. *Please*."

"I'll be back for the bus," he told her.

Liam caught up with the woman along Cable Street. She laughed off the incident as an innocent mistake, returning the lighter without hassle.

At the bus stop, Liam found his sports bag where he'd left it. On top, his hoodie was neatly-folded. Rosie and her rucksack had gone.

He sat on the shelter seat, head and heart numbed by the cold. He should call the landlord, get back into the pub, or he could call a taxi and still catch Rosie at the station.

Why hadn't she waited?

Seems a bit flaky.

Mam would have an answer. Liam opened the scrapbook, stroking her grainy cheek as he talked. The drizzle became solid, determined rain. A lone car veered close to the kerb, spraying dirty water towards Liam's trainers.

Watch yourself.

From inside his jacket, Liam's mobile rang. It vibrated, dancing above his chest like a second, and more frantic, heart. He kissed Mam's paper-thin forehead. "Face of an angel," he said out loud to nobody in particular.

TWISTED

Granddad was having a bit of a turn. Mum didn't want a gaggle of giggling little girls upsetting him. Her party was cancelled and Alice had to be grown up about it. The doctor had called earlier and now Granddad needed peace and quiet. Alice picked the eight candles off the birthday cake one by one, licking the pink fondant icing from the spikes of the plastic holders. Under Mum's direction, she cut a wedge out of the plain Victoria sponge, lipstick-red jam sticking to her fingers.

"A nice big slice," said Mum, her long, flat, brown hair falling forward over her shoulders. "This is for Granddad, remember. He loves my sponge cake."

"Pigs will eat anything," said Auntie Ruth. Her hand rested gently on the back of Alice's head. "Don't you think the birthday girl should get first dibs on her own cake?" She mouthed something to Mum, something like *stop putting the stinking old goat first*. Alice loved Auntie Ruth, because she said exactly what she was thinking, even if it was a bit rude.

Auntie Ruth had made a special trip, because it was Alice's birthday, and was staying for the whole week. This made up for the party being cancelled. It made up for a lot.

"You can take it in to Granddad." Mum toppled the slice onto a pink paper plate, holding it out to Alice. "Ruthie will bring along his cup of tea in a minute."

Granddad lived on the ground floor in what used to be the dining room. A big square room with double doors that could open out onto the patio, but never did. Heavy, mud-brown drapes kept the sun away. Alice thought his room always smelled of wee. With his metal three-legged frame, Granddad could just about get around unsupervised. He could hobble to the downstairs loo, but he often left the door open. Once she'd caught sight of his pyjama bottoms pooling around his slippers, as he stood before the toilet. She'd squeezed her eyes tight. A motorised chair carried him upstairs to the main bathroom, where Mum had fitted a special bath seat that went up and down like the stair lift. Alice liked playing with the bath seat, whizzing Benjy the cat up and down, until Mum caught her and slapped the back of her legs.

He was usually napping when she was sent to his room on some errand. Propped up on pillows, mouth drooping and the remains of his last meal dribbling down his chin. She could creep in and out without having to go near the bed. That afternoon, he was awake. He blinked at her.

"How about a birthday kiss?" Granddad tapped a shaky finger on his purple-streaked cheek.

She had to lean on the knobbly, custard-coloured bedspread to kiss him. Alice felt the scratch of bristles on her lips. A wrinkled hand snaked up under the frilly hem of the new party dress Mum was letting her wear all day, since it was her birthday.

A strangled screech came from behind her. Auntie Ruth had followed with the promised cup of tea. The cup and saucer fell to the carpet, splashing lukewarm tea across the pink satin of Alice's dress. The cake slid from its plate, falling into jammy clumps on her ballet pumps.

"What about your dad, Alice? I asked for an early memory of when your family was all together, but you haven't mentioned him." The counsellor's sleek black plait fell forward over her pale blue blouse. The colour suited her. Leena always dressed smartly, skirt or trousers and a simple, plain blouse. "Was your dad still living with you and your mum?"

"Good question." She paused for as long as possible, but Leena had infinite patience, never jumping into the silence. "I hardly remember him. He never said or did anything, like one of those extras hanging around the market in EastEnders." Alice crossed her legs to match Leena's posture. Mirroring was an easy technique to mimic, one she'd pinched from an online guide to active listening. She hoped to annoy her, but so far Leena appeared unmoved by the mockery.

Cupping hands on her navy-blue skirt, Leena continued, "Isn't it possible he was at work? He was running your grandfather's business. That must have kept him away from home a lot of the time." Leena perfectly recalled all their previous meetings, yet never took notes, causing Alice to question whether their conversations were being taped. She could only do that with the client's permission – Alice was pretty certain about that.

"S'pose. I do remember something – he used to shoot squirrels in the woods. Once he brought back a squirrel's tail. The stump was bloody and gristly, where he'd cut it off." She shuddered. "It was rank."

Leena's gaze flicked away, above Alice's head. The tickless clock was mounted on the wall behind Alice.

"My head feels like when your headphone leads get all knotted together in a drawer." Alice propped her feet on the edge of the low table that sat between them. "I tug them apart. This happened and then that happened... Aunt Ruth came home for the party that never happened... she fought with Mum. Granddad died. Then the police arrived–" Her foot almost nudged Leena's mug, hand painted with *Mummy* in childish clumsy letters "–when I go back to the drawer, the leads are tangled again."

Leena moved the mug away from Alice's foot. "Sometimes we recall exactly what we want or need to, but usually only when we are ready to remember. It's like pulling at a loose thread and then an entirely different string of memories comes tumbling out. The subconscious does a good job of protecting us by burying or hiding painful memories."

"Brilliant," said Alice, "so my subconscious could be hiding something even more disturbing."

"That's what we're here to find out."

Alice, tired of the game, leaned back in her chair. "I don't want to talk about my dad, not today."

Leena nodded. "Tell me about your community service."

"Like what?" Alice looked away from Leena. There were no pictures on the walls, no family photographs on display, no knick-knacks on the bookshelves. The walls were a pale mint green matching the carpet. The only personal item in Leena's office was the coffee mug. She didn't have to talk. They could sit in silence for the hour, but Alice had been warned this would mean an extension, more sessions would be scheduled and then more again, if necessary. "We've spent the last three weeks digging bloody ditches. It's been mind-numbing."

"How are you getting on with the rest of the group?"

Alice laughed. "You'd love them: they're a therapist's dream. I don't want to talk about them."

"We don't have to talk about them," said Leena. "Would you like to talk about your granddad's death?"

"That's a closed question!" Alice said with triumph. Leena rarely slipped up on the basics. "I'll let you off for once. Go on, ask me another." She pulled her feet off the table, making the coffee mug tremble.

Alice knew the interrogator's check-list of open questions always began with: how, who, what, when…

How did Granddad come to drown in the bath?

Who was responsible?

How did that make you feel? (One of Leena's favourites.)

What did you do to make your mother hate you?

When did you come to terms with your aunt being arrested for murder?

"You are here because you emptied your grandfather's ashes onto a bedspread and then tried to burn them," said Leena.

Auntie Ruth would have fired back the perfect retort, with appropriate sarcasm. "Along with all the other indiscretions embarrassing my mother," said Alice. "Don't forget I also nick fags and skive school."

"The resulting fire in your mum's bedroom could have burned the house down, Alice. What did you hope to achieve?"

Alice snatched up the painted mug and hurled it over Leena's head. It hit behind the desk, broke instantly, splattering cold coffee across the empty green wall.

Later, at the graffiti-plastered bus stop, she thought how the dripping coffee had looked like one of those inkblot pictures you had to describe. Concentrating her thoughts on the stain, Alice tried to forget the counsellor's wide, hurt eyes as Leena had remained motionless in her seat.

Alice sat with her shoulders pressed against the bedroom door. Benjy's tail twitched a silent beat as he slept in her lap. The voices of Mum and Auntie Ruth carried down the hallway, mainly because they were shouting. It was Granddad's bath night; Alice stayed well clear of this weekly event.

"Daddy would like you to bathe him tonight." Mum's voice was shrill and spiky. Alice could picture her standing rigid with soapy hands on hips. "It wouldn't hurt for you to help out with him around here. Just once, before you bugger off and leave me alone again."

Auntie Ruth's reply echoed round the house. "I'm not bathing that old git." More words flew at Mum, most of them sounded rude, but few made any sense. Sometimes adults talked another language. "You shouldn't leave an old man lying in a bath without supervision, Rachel, God forbid he slips under and can't get up. You'd better get back in there, before he has an accident."

"Were those your aunt's exact words? Did she describe your grandfather as an 'old git', or is this what you now imagine she would call him?" Leena swivelled round to take a sip from the cup of water, a plastic cup, Alice noted, placed on the desk behind her. She wore a white blouse, an emerald silk scarf and tailored black trousers that accentuated her tiny waist.

"Is either relevant?" Alice stared at the wall, where the faint outline of last month's outburst lingered. "What difference does it make to how I feel now?" Her latest distraction was to see how long she could keep the rally going. But Leena was an expert and the game grew dull.

"What happened when the police came for your aunt? Can you tell me what you remember?"

Alice relaxed into the tub chair, crossing her long legs. "Benjy was on the windowsill in my bedroom. I watched them walk her out to the car. Auntie Ruth's hands were handcuffed and the policewoman tugged her forwards. She put a hand on Auntie Ruth's head and pushed her down roughly inside. The next time I saw Auntie Ruth was three months ago, nine years later, when she came to stay with Mum and me."

"After she'd been released?"

"Obviously. It took her two years to pluck up courage and come visit us. I'm glad she did."

Alice had been honest with Leena about her memories. The more she tugged on them, the more they twisted together. Was she remembering Auntie Ruth's arrest frame by frame, as it happened, or replaying a childhood diet of TV police dramas?

A strand of blonde hair came loose as Ruth leant across to kiss her cheek. Alice thought her aunt's new look, a neat blonde bob, was pretty trendy and longed to touch the velvet band of shaven darker hair at the base of her neck. Aunt Ruth's skin smelled of freshly-picked strawberries, but her breath held the sweet and sour of rotting apples.

"How would you like to come on holiday with me? Just the two of us for a couple of weeks," whispered Ruth. Alice nodded fiercely. "Your mum can cope with Granddad and we can have fun." Auntie Ruth's eyes were bright, her smile filling the room. "Tomorrow morning I'll sort out the details and we can start packing."

She tucked the duvet under Alice's arms and kissed her again, this time on her centre parting. Alice thought this was the final goodnight kiss, but her aunt sank gently onto the bed beside her, squashing the tip of Benjy's tail. He mewed in complaint and moved further down to curl on Alice's feet. Looking round the room, decorated in a monochrome pink palette, Auntie Ruth added, "Not all little girls have to be princesses. You can choose whatever you want to be. If you want to wear scarlet or paint your room black, that's okay with me." She started to get up, but sat straight down again and squeezed Alice's hand. "The angels and I will look out for you, Alice. And remember, not all angels have wings you can see."

The next morning, Alice heard strange voices downstairs, so she stopped at the bend in the staircase, beside the arched window. Curled like a comma on the glossy sill was her favourite way to sit, watching the weather roll over the South Downs. Alice clambered up in time to see Auntie Ruth and a policewoman walk out to the police car. The policewoman's hand rested on the back of Auntie Ruth's denim jacket, as if guiding her forward. Auntie Ruth gripped her handbag in small white hands.

Leena made an audible sigh. "So, there were no handcuffs. Your aunt walked unrestrained to the police car."

"In each version, the picture changes. I can't help that!" Alice snapped back, then mumbled, "Thought these sessions were supposed to drag out the truth."

"These sessions are to help you with your anger, to understand why you need to lash out."

"I know why," Alice said sharply. She breathed out and then smirked. "What I really want is to stop chucking coffee mugs at people."

Leena examined her nails; they were glossed, but unpainted, edged by crisp crescent moons. "Why do you think you need to lash out?"

Alice stood. What was the point of carrying on with this farce, when clearly Leena never listened? Her mother was a bully and Auntie Ruth had been a fucking lunatic fixated with angels, before she upgraded to a drunk.

"We still have another five minutes," said Leena in a quiet, contained voice. She didn't blink, but her cheek muscles tightened.

Alice jabbed at the fading bruise on her own cheek. "Why don't you ask why Mum did this?" With her hand on the door handle, she turned back briefly. "Why don't you ask me what happened after Auntie Ruth kissed me goodnight and before the police arrived in the morning?"

If Leena asked that question, then maybe she would finally remember for herself. Auntie Ruth refused to fill in the gaps, refused to talk about that time.

Leena didn't move from her seat, which was a shame, as Alice wanted to see the woman's shoulder blades. To check for sprouting wing buds beneath the white cotton blouse.

The Lawsons' midsummer barbecue was legendary in Alice's cul-de-sac. Each year, she secretly pretended that the party food and decorations were all for her – in honour of the birthday her mum no longer celebrated. The cake table wobbled under the weight of the chocolate fountain, lemon meringue tartlets and mini éclairs. Chinese lanterns and outdoor lights were woven around the large garden like Santa's summer grotto. Adults swatted away the circling wasps above Mr Lawson's homemade, and definitely not-for-kids, punch.

When she was younger, Alice had commandeered the trampoline, ring-fenced with netting, as her happy place. She kicked off her sandals and bounced until she almost threw up, not caring who saw her knickers as her summer dress leapt with her into the blue sky. This year, the barbecue was timed to coincide with the celebrations for the Lawsons' twenty-fifth wedding anniversary. Using her weekly allowance, Alice had bought a new dress, which showed off her waxed, tanned legs. A manic, bald-headed clown replaced the bouncy castle as the children's entertainment, although his inappropriate squirting from a fake flower down the cleavage of several mothers wouldn't secure him a return gig. Alice, now in her teens, was too big for the trampoline, which sat forlorn and forgotten at the bottom of the garden, damp rose petals pooling in its saggy centre.

"Not bouncing today, Alice?" said Mr Lawson, standing way too close. He breathed beer and fried onions across the back of her neck. "I loved watching you on the trampoline. You always look so happy, trying to touch the sky."

"Don't you think I'm a bit old to be playing on trampolines, Mr Lawson?"

Handing Alice a plastic wine glass, almost overflowing with punch, he winked overtly, saying, "A pretty girl is never too old to flash her knickers. And you are old enough now, Alice, to call me Peter."

She shifted her weight, slouching away from him, and a thin strap slid off her bare shoulder. Alice suddenly wished she had worn a bra under the skin-tight scarlet dress. His fingers were warm and smooth against her skin, as they gently rolled the loose strap back into place. Since Auntie Ruth had gone away, nobody ever touched her. Alice's only human contact was the occasional shove as somebody pushed her out of the way in the school corridors. Hours later, lying on top of her duvet, with Benjy curled into her side, she could still feel the weight and warmth of Mr Lawson's touch on her shoulder, glowing like a fluorescent handprint in the dark.

"I'm confused by the timeline, Alice. Is this a recent barbecue?" Leena's voice had a cool edge. She wove fingers together, clenching her hands.

"It was last year."

"How old were you?"

Alice shrugged. "Fifteen or sixteen, I guess."

Leena was wearing heavy, black-rimmed glasses, making her brown eyes seem rounder than usual. She hadn't worn them at any of their previous appointments and Alice wondered if Leena normally used disposable lenses. She was finding it hard to keep eye contact, her attention continually drawn to the shiny, ebony arms of the glasses hooked behind Leena's perfectly shaped ears.

"Were you underage?"

"No, the party must have been mid-July or later as it was celebrating their wedding anniversary. My sixteenth birthday had already happened." She wriggled on the sticky chair, causing the leopard print mini-skirt to ride up her bare legs, making an uncomfortable squeak.

"Your next-door neighbour, Peter Lawson, seduced you during a party for his twenty-fifth wedding anniversary?"

"Don't you believe me?"

"I want to be clear on the facts, Alice."

"We did it on my mum's bed. I had to shoo Benjy off first. Then he, Peter that is, put a towel over the duvet."

"A towel?"

"In case I bled." Alice put her feet up onto the low coffee table that kept them apart. "He was being practical, you see."

Natural daylight was leaking from the room, the sky darkening from white to grey then finally to black. At first, the patter of rain on glass was gentle and haphazard like an afterthought, but grew quickly to a frenzied battering of tiny, determined hailstones.

"It was your first time?"

"Shocking, huh?" Alice studied her own nails, uneven, plain and grubby. "That I was still a virgin by my sixteenth birthday."

"Did he get you drunk? You said he gave you punch."

"No. I didn't touch a drop, was sober for the whole experience, which didn't last long."

Peter Lawson's mouth stretched into a misshapen grimace, his eyes scrunched shut as he arched away from her. His breathing juddered, spluttering like a failing engine, making Alice think he was about to have a heart attack. But then he cried out loudly and slumped forwards gasping, a landed fish upon her chest. She dug her nails into his naked back, probing into muscle and fat. Alice couldn't feel anything beneath the flabby skin.

"Tell me more about this fascination for angels," Leena asked, her voice uncharacteristically soft. "Does this come from Auntie Ruth?"

Alice tucked her knees onto the chair, clasping her hands around them. "I haven't found one yet." She bowed her head, resting her chin on her knees, as if in prayer. "I lied."

Leena leant forwards. "Lied about what?"

The leads untangled, spiralling apart. The drawer in her head was suddenly neat and tidy, each memory distinct and catalogued, just waiting for inspection. The bathroom door swung backwards as Alice leant against it. Granddad was slumped on the bath seat; a whistling sound came from his open mouth. He'd fallen asleep in the soapy water.

"Benjy," said Alice, lifting her head again. "I lied about Benjy. We never had a cat. Mum hated animals."

Leena gently touched the corner of one eye as if brushing away an eyelash. "I understand why you needed to create him. We all need someone or something to cherish."

Alice tried to scratch at the itch pushing through her shoulder blades. She gave up and slid from the chair onto the green carpet.

Her mum was now shouting at Auntie Ruth on the landing. "Why make such a fuss, Ruth? Daddy loves Alice."

"Like he loved me?" Auntie Ruth's voice was almost a shriek.

"You always got special treatment, all the attention. And then you made up all those hateful stories."

There was a loud crack and a thud as someone fell against the wall. Had Auntie Ruth hit Mum? Alice bumped into the bath, her bobbly dressing gown hooking onto the seat mechanism. The safety catch was off.

There was another slapping sound. "You and Mummy never believed me. I'm taking Alice away, before he starts it all over again."

Alice didn't understand what they were arguing about. She tugged her dressing gown free from the control panel; the bath seat began to whirr. Granddad's purple face sank under the water, his yellow-tipped fingers slipping and sliding against the plastic sides of the pink bath. He seemed unable to pull himself back up again.

She was too scared to call for help. If Mum found her there, then she wouldn't be allowed to go on holiday with Auntie Ruth.

The water sloshed over the sides of the bath, making little puddles on the tiles. Granddad was still under the surface, his eyes now open, staring up at the ceiling. He'd stopped thrashing about. A hand stroked the top of her head. Auntie Ruth was at her side.

"Go back to bed, Alice," said Auntie Ruth softly. "I'll look after Granddad."

THE FROST HARE

The moon is fat and happy. Its light drips onto the graves like molten silver. I warm my hands with hot breaths in the frost-filled air. My bottom is perched on the smooth curve of Edith's marble headstone. Edith died six years before I came to England, a devoted wife to John, yet in the quiet of the night she patiently listens to my stories of Ana. Together, Edith and I, we wait for the frost hare. I know she will come this one last time.

*

"Your English is good," Jacob said. Slipping me a chocolate bar, he added, "I can spare a couple, perks of the job."

Jacob peddled magazines and sweet distractions to the friends and family who wandered the corridors like lost spirits. I whispered prayers for the dying, mopped floors and re-filled water jugs for the living. It was only my second day in the ICU and already death was a nodding acquaintance.

"In Bucharest I watched English movies," I told him. "The old black and white films were the best. Celia Johnson in Brief Encounter spoke so beautifully." Breaking off a chunk of chocolate, I offered it back to Jacob, only later realising this gesture of friendship was a mistake. He took it as flirtation. The crowd of white coats around the girl's bed was moving on and I needed to clean her room. "I'd better get back to work," I said.

Jacob held out his hand for another piece of chocolate. "Why the hurry? She's not going anywhere."

"What's wrong with her?"

The girl looked younger than me, mid-twenties. Thin, bare arms were the same starched white as her bed sheet. She slept all day, long silver blonde hair combed neatly over each shoulder, rising and falling with her breasts.

"We've christened her Aurora, after Sleeping Beauty," said Jacob. He paused, waiting for me to nod, but I didn't understand the reference. "The princess from the Disney cartoon? Except our Aurora is in a persistent vegetative state," he continued. "They think she's an illegal. No ID. No name. She was sleeping in a pile of rubbish bags at the bus station. It was probably the only place she could find any warmth. A driver backed a bus over her."

I tested the words out in my head before speaking. "Persistent vegetative state, does that mean she is in a coma?"

"It means that, unlike Sleeping Beauty, she will never wake up, not even with a kiss."

If she had been living rough, that explained the absence of visitors at her bedside. Relatives normally lined the open ward like sentries, some chatting, some reading, ever hopeful for the return of their loved ones from the abyss. The girl in the coma would sleep on for eternity, with no-one waiting on her return.

It was already dark by the end of that second shift, but I still took the shortcut home through St Jude's churchyard. Ana had shown me the quiet beauty of graveyards, how only peace haunted the shy spaces between headstones and sculptured angels. There was nothing to fear from the dead. *Only the living can hurt us*, she told me, only days before her husband found us together.

The moon was a skinny sliver peeking out from black sheets. The night air held its breath and grass crunched underfoot as I veered off the gravel path to visit Edith. Brushing off a dusting of frost from her headstone, I sat and took out a cigarette. "My first today," I said aloud to silence.

At the sound of my voice, a shadow twitched, then instantly turned itself to stone. I held the unlit cigarette between my fingers and stared unblinking into the gloom. My eyes gradually adjusted, as the crouching outline of an animal grew in definition. It was too long for a rabbit and the quivering ears, stretched low across the animal's back, could only belong to a hare. We watched each other, trembling as the ice crystals melted on our skin and fur. Then the hare leapt behind a lopsided tomb and was gone. I sat for several minutes without lighting up the cigarette, as I thought the smell would keep the animal away, but she didn't return. Though I majored in literature, not the natural sciences, I recognised a kindred spirit and instinctively knew the hare was a female. I had glimpsed the ache of loss in her eyes.

Each day I cleaned Aurora's room and finished by pulling the blind shut so I could wipe down the slats. Before leaving, I sat on the bed and brushed her hair. I talked in Romanian, telling her what I planned to cook later that evening, usually pasta, cheap and quick. The girl's fine hair shone against the crisp linen pulled tight across her. Her gold-tipped lashes sometimes twitched as if she were dreaming, but her eyes never opened.

Jacob intercepted me at the nurses' station as I pulled on my jacket. He waved a leaflet. "Casablanca – that must count as one of your black and white classics, huh? There's a special showing tonight in town. How about it?"

Thinking quickly, I reasoned that I could still walk back through the graveyard after the film. Visiting Edith and the hare were now part of my daily routine. After turning Jacob down for several drinks, coffee in the canteen and finally a home-cooked Sunday lunch, it was time to end this one-sided dance.

After the film, I would explain the problem.

"Okay," I said it quickly. "I would like that, Jacob."

He fingered the plait coiled at the nape of my neck. "You could wear your hair down. I'd like that."

My smile stretched to breaking point. Perhaps, it would be safer not to meet him after all. I decided to text him later with some excuse for not turning up. I couldn't risk another rejected man ruining my life.

Jacob hadn't replied to my apologetic text, so I lingered longer than usual at Edith's grave, unwilling to walk home in case he knew where to wait for me. I told her I'd chosen the UK for my new home after the accident, because of Celia Johnson's refined English manners. In my imagination, Edith replied with Celia's clipped vowels. She scolded me for living too long amongst the dead.

Leaving Bucharest before the verdict had been announced meant I never knew if the charge of death by dangerous driving had imprisoned Ana's husband. Yes, I could easily check this online, but it was less painful to keep hiding from the truth. Without Ana, I didn't really care if he had been punished or not. What did it matter? I thought of Aurora in the hospital: like me, she too was alone. Nobody missed her absence in the world.

The hare followed my trail of raisins, pausing between each treat to scent the air and twitch her long silken ears. Her tolerance of me grew with her confidence, as each night she crept closer. I crouched on my heels, a raisin offered in a flat palm. She stretched towards the tips of my fingers. I felt the tickle of her whiskers and hesitant sniffs. The hare tested my finger with her teeth and licked at my palm.

From beyond the church came the sharp, stiff bark of a fox. When I looked down again, both hare and raisin had disappeared.

*

The front wheel of Jacob's trolley clipped, my bucket spilling soapy water across the corridor. "Oops," he said, without stopping.

The blinds were up in Aurora's room, so I smiled in at her, told her she was the most beautiful creature I'd ever seen. The frost hare, delicate and poised, was her only rival. Stroking her hair, I bent closer, felt the whisper of breath on my cheek, and then gently touched her lips with mine.

I waited as dusk drifted towards night and then on until dawn, but the hare did not come to the graveyard. By sunrise, I could barely move my legs to walk back to the hospital for the first shift. The woollen gloves were dank and damp with melting frost and my hands clenched inside like crooked claws.

In the ICU, an orderly was making up Aurora's bed. The drip tube, the monitors and wires were gone.

The room was bare.

The guy plumped pillows into place. He asked kindly, "What's up, love?"

"The girl in the coma, she was in this room, where is she?"

He shrugged, tugging the clean sheet under the mattress. "Dunno, love."

I ran out of the room. Jacob would know what had happened to Aurora. Jacob knew everything.

He was in the visitors' lounge, spooning a teabag into the bin. "Where is she?" I cried. "Is she... has she...?"

Something flared in his eyes. The same look Ana's husband had shared with me.

Ana died on the way to hospital. Ana is... Ana...

"They had to move her," Jacob said, adding milk to the mug.

"Why?" The English words stuck inside me. My knees were failing; I was about to fall and once on the ground, I would begin to howl. "Why did they move her from the ICU?"

His eyes were cold. "Because she woke up."

*

Together, Edith and I wait in the shadow of the swollen moon for the hare. I know she will come this one last time.

A flicker of movement makes me turn to the church, where a shadow sits back onto long legs. The hare stretches towards the sky, her silhouette slowly becomes human. A tall, slender young woman walks towards the graves. Her pale skin swallows the moonlight.

For one frozen breath, I believe it is Ana, returned to me.

The girl carries two red roses; their petals shine like freshly spilled blood. She places one rose on Edith's grave and offers the other to me. Holding its stem, I feel her fingers curl round mine and she breathes frost-laced air into my mouth as we kiss.

GRETEL AND THE CHOCOLATE WOLF

The fire crackled, spitting hot embers onto Gretel's apron as she stirred their supper. She watched the stranger, who stood on the doorstep in her grandmother's scrawny shadow. The soldier stamped his boots and blew into cupped hands. Black hair flopped across his eyes, which squinted through the gloom of the cottage to find Gretel's gaze. He was the first man to stand at the threshold since Gretel's father had left.

"My son, Hansel, walked out fifteen summers ago," said the old woman to the shivering youth. "Joined the militia, leaving me his wife and daughter to feed and house. Now I have just Gretel. The villagers leave us alone. Nobody comes this deep into the forest. So no, there are no men for you to commission here." She added with a snort, "And we have no food to spare."

The soldier held up a copper coin and leant towards the inner glow of the parlour. Gretel's eyes blazed, reflecting the flames that licked at the charred base of the swinging pot.

"We have no need of money," spat the grandmother. She lifted the door and heaved against it till the latch fell, clicking shut. "I knew, one day, another wolf would come sniffing round." Hobbling over to the hearth, she pinched Gretel's wrist with bony fingers and hissed through broken teeth, "Remember what happened to your mother, girl. Stay away from the wolf."

Gretel's night was haunted by strange dreams of the young soldier. He called on her, wearing tailored clothes that no longer dripped over his bent body, but instead clung to his tight, muscular frame. He stood tall and straight, his face was clean-shaven and wavy, long hair shone like a raven's wing. Carrying a fistful of lilac flowers, picked fresh from the meadow, he serenaded Gretel with sweet, mournful songs of love.

The soldier returned to the cottage as dusk swept away the dregs of the next day. Gretel first glimpsed the long outline of his trench coat as he slouched against the chicken hut, before catching his pale face staring out from the shadows.

"My men are hungry, Gretel; they need meat," said the boy. In the half-light, she could see he was barely a summer older than her.

"Grandmother warns that snow is coming. That your men will perish if you don't move on."

Grey teeth grinned out from behind the wiry beard that curled around his mouth. He glanced up to the sky, shrouded beneath a grubby veil of stagnant clouds. "It's too warm and cloudy for snow," he laughed back at her. "Your grandmother's curses are as weak as my heart." One hand slid from behind his back; it held the limp carcass of a hen. "I wanted to give you some payment before I took this." His other hand held out a slab of something that looked like mud, wrapped in stiff brown paper.

Gretel stared at the offering.

"Chocolate," said the soldier, "army rations, but it's good. Taste it." As Gretel reached for his open palm, the boy snatched back his hand. "But I need one more thing," he whispered, leaning towards her, breath stinking of sour beer. Then cold, damp lips pressed onto her mouth. His tongue pushed inside, rasping and probing. With the hen still grasped tight, he fumbled underneath her cloak to roughly squeeze her breasts.

After the kiss, Gretel bit into a sliver of the chocolate. Bitter and sweet at the same time, it seemed to swell like soaking corn and fill her mouth, sticking to teeth and tongue like rich black treacle. She breathed its cloying scent and then shoved in a whole square. "It tastes like midnight," said Gretel, flicking her tongue across chocolate-stained fingertips.

"You can have more," he laughed. "Tomorrow I can bring more chocolate, but what will you offer me in return?" Lank hair fell again into dark eyes.

"At noon, my grandmother leaves the cottage to gather kindling. She is old and her legs are slow. There will be time for many kisses."

He nodded. And, lifting the hem of her woollen skirt with the toe of his boot, added, "I will need more than kisses, pretty Gretel."

Inside the cottage, the old woman squeezed Gretel's lips together. Sniffing her granddaughter's mouth, she growled, "You smell of wolf, girl." Gretel knew what was coming next. She knew the words by heart, like an old song they echoed inside her head as the crone began the tale. "That winter we wore our bones on the outside. The sun deserted the forest while we lived a half-life, frozen in a white shroud. Everything we owned fed the hungry fire, while we slowly starved, waiting for death to creep softly through the snow. And yet your mother remained rosy and round. Each evening she returned from the forest, plump like a brooding hen. Then, one day, the wolf followed her to the cottage and gobbled her up. I saved you, girl, with a single shot. Your father's hunting musket killed that feasting wolf dead."

"He's not a wolf," Gretel said, staring into the fire.

"They're all wolves," her grandmother snarled back.

The soldier returned as promised, first waiting for Gretel's grandmother to set off into the forest and then striding up to rap on the mottled glass of the cottage's solitary window. A fresh slab of chocolate peeked from the pocket of his long coat.

His beard had been trimmed down to scratchy bristles and his tongue tasted of stale stewed meat. Gretel let him pull away the dirty linen underskirts to roam scarred hands across her skin; with closed eyes she thought again of the dream lover. The solider grunted and rooted over her body like a truffling pig.

At dusk, the old woman found the lovers asleep in Gretel's bed. Retrieving the well-oiled musket from its hook, she then gently unfurled the boy's skeletal frame from her granddaughter's arms. Gretel woke too slowly to save the wolf from her grandmother's wrath.

Together they folded the soldier into his long coat, and bound him tightly to the wooden slats. Gretel trudged behind, as her grandmother pulled the sled, its polished runners gouging a trail in the settling snow. Dark blood trickled from the dead boy's mouth as his head lolled back and forth. The forest creaked around them, skinny winter branches growing heavy the farther they walked.

The old woman sang, as Gretel scraped out a shallow ditch in the black earth. Gretel did not understand the strange words of her grandmother's song, but the eery, wailing notes weaved pictures of ancient lands and the long dead. Like cold mountain water, the shapeless words seeped into her heart, freezing it solid.

The soldier's blue face and fish eyes stared out as they rolled him into the grave. Gretel shovelled earth quickly on top, to obscure his surprise. But then she remembered his promise. "The chocolate," cried Gretel, "it's still in his pocket!"

Her grandmother entwined a loose golden curl of Gretel's hair and tugged it sharply, making the girl whimper. "Leave it, if you wish to see him again." Her voice suddenly sweetened, "Do you wish to see the chocolate wolf again?"

Gretel watched the cruel smile slither across her grandmother's cracked lips. "Yes," she said, without hesitation.

The parlour glowed from the moonlight streaming into the cottage. Gretel crouched by the feeble fire, listening to the rattle of the old woman's snores. A rap of knuckles on glass stirred Gretel from her dozing, dream world. She looked to the window where a lone figure stood.

Gretel hung up his damp, heavy coat to steam by the fire. Moonbeams curved around the soldier's body like a silver halo. The sores and flea scabs were gone, healed beneath the smooth outer varnish of the youth's new coating. She scratched a fingernail across his sculptured cheek and hungrily licked up the flakes falling like chocolate dust. They lay down together on the straw covered floor and the soldier's hands stroked the girl's skin, as if brushing her with kidskin gloves. Gretel bit his fingertips and devoured first one earlobe, then the next. His perfect body gleamed, like polished ebony, and she tasted all of him.

When the pink tendrils of dawn slivered through the frozen forest, the old woman shuffled from her bed. Her granddaughter sat alone in the hearth, the soldier's coat draped around her naked body like the pelt of a giant grey wolf.

"So your chocolate wolf returned?"

The girl answered only with a sly smile. Her curls tumbled over the coat's faded lapels, glinting as if glazed with golden honey and her clear blue eyes shone bright like a summer's sky. Dipping the old woman's drinking cup into the bubbling pot of liquid midnight, Gretel lightly traced the tip of her tongue over the smudged brown line ringing her rosebud lips, and said, "Look Grandmother, I've made hot chocolate."

WOOD

Richard watched the flame burn black, as the final candle's wick sank to the base of the flimsy tea light. The other four were already garish green puddles, remnants of last Christmas, dug out hastily to illuminate the evening.

"There's sorbet for pudding," said Sarah, leaning across the heavy tang of wilting pine to take Richard's plate.

"I love your lemon sorbet," he replied.

"Shop bought. Sorry. Didn't have time." Her words burbled like a burst pipe.

Richard dabbed his lips with a linen serviette, one of six, wedding gifts from her parents and embroidered with their entwined initials. "Still a 'yes' to the sorbet. Shall I make coffee?"

"If you like." Sarah was already carrying the dishes to the kitchen. Flat, still damp hair dripped towards the curve of her back, the tangled ends, over-long and splitting.

"How about an early night?" he called out hopefully.

Her voice echoed back from the kitchen, "I'd prefer to watch some telly, relax for a bit. It's been a hell of a day. I'm shattered, but not ready for bed yet."

Richard picked up the new pepper grinder, almost a foot high, polished and gleaming like an ebony phallic totem. Was his wife's anniversary gift a comment on his emotional intelligence, implying his inner life was static, immobile as a dense, dark forest? Or was she just taking the piss out of his manhood?

"We needed a replacement," Sarah had stated, "and it is made of wood. Five years is the wooden anniversary."

"Oh. I didn't know that."

He should have played her at her own game; presented a tray of ice cubes, carefully wrapped in scented tissue paper, instead of the exorbitantly expensive bra and knickers set he'd chosen late that afternoon. The bra cups, or what masqueraded as support, were too small. *Apparently.* How could he know her cup size, when he rarely penetrated the perimeter petticoat?

The jingle of cutlery and slap of plates signalled Sarah was loading the dishwasher. Richard waited for her to return with the sorbet, not technically a pudding, more of a palate-cleansing head freeze.

"Prefer to watch telly, huh?" he muttered. Anticipating his wife's lack-lustre libido, Richard had a contingency plan ready for execution. In the gloom, he slit open the sachet with a steak knife and tipped half the contents into his glass. The other half went into Sarah's untouched Merlot. Richard swilled the crystal goblet to dissolve the clear, stringy droplets. He drank the rest of his wine quickly. Sharp and stringent, it burned the back of his throat. Maybe he should've pushed the boat out a little further and picked up some bubbly. Prosecco used to work a treat on Sarah's underwear.

"Can I help?" he called out.

"No." She swung back through the door with two dishes, one in each hand. "I can manage." Sarah's voice lightened, "Where did you pick up the roses, the supermarket?"

"Don't you like them?"

Two yellow spheres of sorbet, suns in miniature, squatted in the cereal bowl she placed before him. Richard felt the crack of ice at the edge of his spoon. The CD had ended. Neither of them moved to restart or replace it.

"Somebody's cocked up big time." She smirked, letting out a hiccup. "The sachet of nutrients that came with the roses — it does a lot more sustaining than normal." Richard blinked, as the room began to drift out of focus. Sarah tossed an empty black packet onto the tablecloth. *"Put the sex back into your romance,"* she said and giggled. "I don't know what I've just emptied into the flower vase but I think it's supposed to do more than stiffen their stems."

He could no longer reply, mouth clogged with twigs and leaf litter, and his throat crackled, studded with musty bark.

"Some idiot's muddled up the packets; whether by accident or for a joke, but it appears your half dozen blooms came with a sachet of love juice. What a hoot!" Sarah knelt beside him, rhythmically stroking the material of his trousers.

A dank coldness like ancient roots pushed down through his chest, down through his static legs, through his socks, through the soles of his feet into the thick cream carpet.

"I'm feeling more relaxed now," whispered Sarah. "Why don't you bring the rest of the wine upstairs and we can have that early night after all? I'll just go up and change."

Richard couldn't raise his head to watch her leave, unable to twist or turn his thick, solid neck. She hadn't spotted the other, empty sachet, the one that had come with the flowers, the one he'd picked up in haste. Around him, the house settled quietly, cooling and contracting.

Sarah returned wearing only a petticoat. White satin stretched across the swell of her breasts and belly. Richard felt vindicated: she had put on weight.

"I've been waiting." The girlish giggle had gone. Sarah's mouth was a tight pink line. "Why are you still sitting in the dark?"

Lignin oozed through his veins, leaching beyond capillaries into every cell, coating every synapse. Memories scurried away like deserting rats, leaving Richard oddly relieved. The burden of sentient existence, of responsibility and guilt, would soon be extinguished. He could just *be*.

"I wanted to tell you something tonight," said Sarah, her eyes squinting. "Something important. About us. About our future." Pale hands cradled the curve of her stomach.

A small remembrance of Richard flickered. His seed had fallen on fertile ground.

"You really are a prick." She snatched up the pepper grinder. "I'd get more response from this wooden object. You're sleeping in the spare room tonight, okay!"

The pepper grinder flew over Richard's head, bounced off the wall, and bowled the photograph frame off the mantelpiece into the fireplace, where the glass splintered on the slate tiles, freeing the two startled mannequins from their wedding day pose.

Somewhere, deep inside his trunk, a nerve ending twitched.

JUMPING THE BOX

The taffeta frills of the crimson basque scratch against the box, as I wiggle free my hips. Okay, I confess, I may have put on a few pounds since we first performed this trick. I've doubled in age, so it's hardly surprising my waistline has followed.

Tapping out the score with my fingers, I listen for the violin crescendo as the curtains close to obscure the coffin at the centre of the stage.

Beside every great magician poses a pert, pretty box jumper. Her purpose is to flirt with the audience's attention, to misdirect belief and emerge unscathed from certain death. Behind every great magician hides a trick designer, stage director and con artist. As Sweet Mo (Maureen back-stage), I performed all these roles for over twenty years. Without me, the Great Rondini would still be Ronald Dimchurch, shuffling his card tricks at The Nag's Head. *I can make you believe, darling,* was his pick-up line.

The hiss of gas precedes the whoop of the audience, as the flame bursts into life beneath the rope.

At the press call earlier, Rondini thanked me, his faithful wife, for all the years on stage. I simpered, chuckling on what pleasure I could take from watching my husband slice someone else in half. Miss Honeydew, my replacement in the act, and his affections, stepped into the spotlight, sequins barely covering her assets.

The rack of spikes drops into view behind the curtains. The audience gasps on cue.

When I first devised this trick, I'd planned for the falling spears to pierce bags of theatrical blood at the base of the coffin. Imagine the shocked hush, as the punters believe the trick has gone wrong. Sweet Mo trapped inside the box — a gored and bloody ragdoll. Ron wouldn't have it. "Think of the kiddies," he scolded.

My left hand reaches for the latch, but skims over smooth wood. When the drum roll begins, I scrabble fingers along the panel. I've lost count and no longer know how long is left until the rope burns through and the spikes drop. They are cast iron. Sharpened to a point.

After the music climaxes, Rondini is supposed to winch the rack free of the coffin, only for Miss Honeydew to sit up and wave to the cheering crowd. Finally, I will stumble back on stage in dressing gown and fluffy slippers, already retired from the act.

The bastard has switched boxes. There is no escape latch.

Had he discovered my desertion to the opposition's camp? His act was my creation; the secrets moved with me, would die with me.

The audience rises, clapping and stamping their feet when I appear at my husband's side. The Great Rondini is transfixed, amazed even, his pink cheeks leaching to grey.

The points of the spikes, protruding from the coffin base, drip with scarlet.

Miss Honeydew's debut is short-lived.

I stand on satin tiptoes to whisper in his ear, "Darling, I always believed."

ACKNOWLEDGEMENTS

'Ten Good Reasons', originally published online at Five Stop Story (2011).

'Vector', shortlisted for the 2020 Bridport Prize, winner of 2021 University of Chichester Audio Story Prize, and recorded by The Story Player.

'The Naming of Moths', Regional Winner for Canada and Europe 2017 Commonwealth Short Story Prize, and published online at Granta (2017).

'Coping Mechanism', published in 'I You She He It — Experiments in Viewpoint' (The Grist Anthology, 2017).

'Household Gods', shortlisted for 2014 Commonwealth Short Story Prize, and published in Unthology10 (Unthank Books, 2018).

'In the Copper Canyon', published online at Fictive Dream (2020).

'Ancient Wing', published online at Holdfast magazine (2014) and in 'Rattle Tales 4' anthology (2016).

'Monsters', published in the anthology 'The Colour of Life' (Retreat West, 2013) and online at Pornokitsch (2014).

'The Weight They Left Behind', published online at The Cabinet of Heed (2019).

'Twisted', published in 'New Short Stories 9' (Willesden Herald, 2016).

'The Frost Hare', published in the anthology 'The Brighton Prize 2016'.

'Gretel and the Chocolate Wolf', winner 2012 Steyning Festival Short Story Prize, and published in 'Rattle Tales 2' anthology (2013).

'Wood', published in 'Let Me Tell You A Story' (Waif Sands Publishing, 2016).

AUTHOR BIOGRAPHY

Tracy Fells was the 2017 Regional Winner (Europe and Canada) for the Commonwealth Short Story Prize. Her short fiction has been widely published in print journals and online, including Granta and Brittle Star. She has been shortlisted for the Bridport and Fish Fiction prizes. She is a regular reader for several international story competitions and leads writing workshops on short fiction. Tracy also writes novels and was a finalist in the 2018 Richard & Judy 'Search for a Bestseller' competition. Her debut novella-in-flash Hairy On The Inside (published by Ad Hoc Fiction, 2021) was shortlisted for the 2022 Saboteur and International Rubery Book Awards.

She tweets as @theliterarypig.

Her website is www.tracyfells.com.

About Fly on the Wall Press

A publisher with a conscience.
Political, Sustainable, Ethical.
Publishing politically-engaged, international fiction, poetry and cross-genre anthologies on pressing issues. Founded in 2018 by founding editor, Isabelle Kenyon.

Some other publications:

The Sound of the Earth Singing to Herself by Ricky Ray

We Saw It All Happen by Julian Bishop

Odd as F*ck by Anne Walsh Donnelly

Imperfect Beginnings by Viv Fogel

These Mothers of Gods by Rachel Bower

Sin Is Due To Open In A Room Above Kitty's by Morag Anderson

Fauna by David Hartley

How To Bring Him Back by Clare HM

Hassan's Zoo and A Village in Winter by Ruth Brandt

No One Has Any Intention of Building A Wall by Ruth Brandt

Snapshots of the Apocalypse by Katy Wimhurst

Demos Rising

Exposition Ladies by Helen Bowie

A Dedication to Drowning by Maeve McKenna

The House with Two Letterboxes by Janet H Swinney

Climacteric by Jo Bratten

The State of Us by Charlie Hill

The Unpicking by Donna Moore

Social Media:

@fly_press (Twitter) @flyonthewallpress (Instagram)

@flyonthewallpress (Facebook and TikTok)

www.flyonthewallpress.co.uk